PROPOSITIONED BY THE BILLIONAIRE MOOSE

A HOWLS Romance

EVE LANGLAIS

It's all about the rack.

Copyright © August 2017, Eve Langlais

Cover Art by Yocla Designs © August 2017

Produced in Canada

Published by Eve Langlais

http://www.EveLanglais.com

E-ISBN-13: 978 1988 328 829

Ingram Print ISBN: 978 1988 328 836

Createspace Print ISBN: 978 1549 799 464

All Rights Reserved

Propositioned by the Billionaire Moose is a work of fiction and the characters, events and dialogue found within the story are of the author's imagination and are not to be construed as real. Any resemblance to actual events or persons, either living or deceased, is completely coincidental. If you think you might be a shapeshifting moose, please consider seeing a mental health professional.

No part of this book may be reproduced or shared in any form or by any means, electronic or mechanical, including but not limited to digital copying, file sharing, audio recording, email and printing without permission in writing from the author.

Chapter 1

"You will do it, or else." A claim that lacked the ominous dum-dum-dum soundtrack to go along with it.

"Or else what, old man?" Bryce grew tired of his grandfather's threats. Especially the one ordering Bryce to get married. Marriage was for pussies who got tricked into grounding their dicks for life.

"Don't test me, boy. I will cut you off and give my estate to someone else." The crotchety old man might lie in a bed, his features creased with age, but there was nothing old or weak about his gaze. The icy blue eyes fixed Bryce.

"Bullshit. You're bluffing." The only grandson of the billionaire, Bryce always knew he'd inherit, especially after his mother passed. The threat to cut him off was hollow. Grandfather would leave his legacy to his only living male heir.

"Better start believing, boy. You're not the only person who'd like to get his hands on my fortune." A sizeable fortune built up over decades of good business and lucky investments.

"Yeah, but I'm the only one actually related to you. Don't tell me you're going to leave your *legacy*"—a word spoken with a certain amount of mockery—"to a non-family member. We both know your daddy made it a condition in his will that only a direct descendent could inherit the company."

"You're right. He did. And my daddy also had two kids." Grandfather sounded rather smug.

"Are you referring to Aunt Trixie?" Bryce frowned. His flighty aunt had never married, to the disapproval of the family. She'd also only gotten a lump sum from her daddy. The family empire went to the eldest, and more responsible, child.

"Yes, I'm talking about my sister. Did you know your aunt had a son? Boy is almost the same age as you, as a matter of fact. Also just as arrogant."

The snide comment stiffened Bryce's back. "Since when did she have a kid? And what does it matter if she did? You can't tell me you'd rather leave the company to an unknown nephew than your own grandson."

The old man adopted a coy expression. "A man in my position, facing his mortality, has got to make some decisions, decisions to ensure the future of his legacy. My newfound nephew was overjoyed to find out about me. Turns out Trixie left her kid with the father and never looked back. My nephew never knew he had more family."

"If what he says is even true." With his aunt dead, only a DNA test would validate the claim.

Grandfather shrugged. "He looks just like her."

"Doesn't mean shit and you know it."

"Worried?" The old curmudgeon intentionally taunted. He always knew how to irritate Bryce.

When Bryce was young, Grandfather challenged him to do better at school, implying he was stupid if he got anything under a B+. The hard work that had him graduating top of his class paid off in the form of a brand-new sport BMW. University had netted him a boat. Yet the fact that Bryce had finished his studies with honors didn't mean shit when he joined the family company. Grandfather made him work hard to rise through the ranks because apparently nepotism didn't make for good business decisions.

Until now.

Now grandfather was talking about leaving their company to an outsider. Had he finally turned senile?

"Whoever he is, he knows nothing about the business," Bryce argued.

"He can learn."

Learn what had taken Bryce years? The unfairness of it made him simmer, and the beast inside pawed with a heavy hoof. His nostrils flared. "You're not about to will your fortune to someone with a different last name."

"Rory is receptive to the idea of taking on the family name. Apparently, he and his father don't get along."

"This is bullshit. You can't be seriously thinking about letting a stranger inherit the family business. A business I've been working my ass off for." The words exploded.

"He won't be a stranger for long. You'll be meeting him shortly. He's coming for a visit. I've invited him to stay at the mansion rather than a hotel so we can get to know each other."

"You're letting a stranger come to live here?" Bryce couldn't help but yell. "Are you out of your mind? You know we can't have outsiders here." An outsider might notice strange things, such as wildlife visiting the house in the dead of night.

"He's my sister's kid."

"Might be," Bryce corrected. "And even if he is, what if he's not one of us? What if he doesn't—"

"Shift?" Grandfather said, interrupting. "You're right. I don't know if he's got the family gene. Not exactly something I could broach via emails and phone calls. But we'll know soon enough. Once he's here, we'll have his blood work rushed off to the lab, but we both know a simple sniff test will also do the trick."

Sniff. Sense. Shapeshifters—those that could swap their human guise for their animal self—could usually identify others of their ilk. The human shell couldn't quite mask the animal within, although cologne could make it difficult. But no amount of perfume in the world would stop Bryce from ousting the imposter.

And he had to be an imposter. It seemed a little convenient that this man had suddenly appeared out of nowhere claiming parentage.

Probably another bloody vulture. The media had recently gotten wind of Grandfather's ailing health. As one of the richest men in Canada, the social pages followed him—and his bachelor grandson—closely.

"He'll turn out to be a fraud. You'll see."

"And if he's not? What ever shall I do with two plausible heirs to my fortune?" asked his grandfather, his gaze turning sly. "Perhaps I'll make it easy. Whoever marries first becomes my heir."

"That's preposterous," Bryce sputtered. "You can't force a man to marry for money." Blackmail wasn't a reason to tie himself to one woman for life.

"Then don't marry, but don't come crying at my grave when I'm gone and you're looking for a real job."

"You'll never die. You're too fucking stubborn," he grumbled.

"Tenacious, my boy. A man shouldn't be afraid or too timid to demand what he wants."

"Even if what he wants involves meddling in other people's lives?"

"Don't like my rules? You know where the door is."

The threat his grandfather used anytime they butted heads.

"One of these days, I will walk out," Bryce grumbled.

"Go ahead. I dare you. See what it's like to actually work for a living."

Except Bryce already knew about hard work. Grandfather might accuse him of being lazy, but Bryce worked hard. Fucking hard. He'd done his time in the trenches, learning the business from the ground up. His fingers were callused from work. How dare that old bastard accuse him otherwise.

"I should start my own company," he grumbled under his breath. One with something he'd long had a passion for.

"What's that, boy?"

Instead of replying, Bryce moved away from the bed holding his invalid grandfather. He needed to move away before he said something he'd really regret. He loved his grandfather even if the old man didn't make it easy. But that didn't mean he'd tolerate abuse—or blackmail.

Surely the old man didn't truly intend to make his will contingent on Bryce getting married.

He was too young, still only a buck, with plenty of prancing years left ahead of him before he let some woman throw a noose around his single life.

There has to be a way out of this. A way to stay single—and rich.

Chapter 2

Being single sucks.

Sucked big hairy balls, with which Melanie had no personal experience. Melanie had little experience with men at all. Not for a lack of wanting a man, more because she worried about hurting a man.

As in putting him in a hospital...

Who says he wouldn't like it? her inner voice purred.

No one liked stitches. Hence why she avoided getting close to anyone of the opposite sex, but right about now, a sturdy man might have come in handy to give her a hug and say he'd handle things. Don't misconstrue, she wasn't weak. Melanie could handle stuff on her own; she was just so goddamned tired of it. For once, it would be nice to let someone carry the burden. To say, "Don't worry, I got this." Right about now, she could have used a man who would gladly carry the groceries home.

The list in her hand appeared short enough, but the juice mother insisted on would make it heavy. She also wondered if she'd have enough funds. Her mother's failing health had meant more expenses than usual. More than the meager government checks could handle and she'd long since spent her last actual paycheck.

Some days Melanie was so tired of scrimping every penny she could. Of cutting coupons and dealing with debt collectors. She'd not asked to be burdened with a sick mother, one made ill because she'd pickled her liver her entire life.

At times she railed against fate, a cruel mistress that had Melanie take on the care of her mother at the expense of her own happiness.

I am only twenty-two. Twenty-two and barely kissed. Twenty-two and never made it anywhere past college. Nope. She'd gotten stuck going back home to take care of the woman who had made her life miserable.

Why can't she just die?

I could help it along. A pillow over her face. A dropped toaster in the shower. A little something in her evening cocoa. Except the cocoa sometimes got tossed in her face, so it would be a waste of the expensive drugs.

Sounded cruel? Walk a mile in her shoes. There

was no love between Melanie and her mother. Hadn't been for as far back as Melanie could remember.

Maizie had never been a true parent to Melanie. Ever. Melanie had been taking care of them both since she could walk and feed herself from the damned fridge.

Just her and a mother who hated Melanie because Daddy left the picture. She couldn't have said if Maizie's drinking drove him away or if the drinking came after.

It didn't matter. Melanie was so bloody tired of it.

The cashier rang up the total. "That will be thirty-six forty-two, ma'am." About three dollars more than she had. The embarrassment of having to pull some items from the checkout no longer had the ability to bring heat to her cheeks. It happened all too often. A coupon she tried to use failed or something ended up a little pricier than expected. She yanked out the crackers. There went her breakfast for the week.

After she paid, she grabbed the plastic bags by the handles and hoped they wouldn't split this time. She could carry the two bags easily, not enough food to create any true weight. A good thing seeing as how the store was two miles from home. God forbid she used any money to take a bus.

"Lazy cow. God gave you legs so use them."

God had given her claws, too, but she kept them sheathed.

As a car swept by, a big white sedan, the windows tinted and closed, with climate control, she sighed.

What would it be like to have money? Not just any money, big money. The kind that meant never looking at a price tag when you shopped. The kind that could hire a nurse for her mother. Or, even better, stick her mother in a home—and bribe the staff to give her daily enemas plus feed her peas. Maizie hated peas.

When she'd had a rough day and couldn't sleep, she liked to fantasize about what she'd do if she had money. The best she could hope for was to win the lottery to make those dreams come true.

A girl like Melanie—born in poverty, with a diploma in hospitality, and a face that never went further than pretty—would never marry a man who drove a luxury car. Especially since she had a secret. A furry secret that added a layer of difficulty in her search for a man.

I am not one hundred percent human. An admission she never made out loud, but she couldn't exactly deny it to herself.

I can change shapes. She didn't know why.

Most likely she'd gotten her special side from her daddy because her mother certainly wasn't a shapeshifter like Melanie. The one time she'd asked, her mother had slapped her so hard and accused her of being a druggie, she'd hissed and almost swiped back.

What if I am wrong? What if the times she went into the woods and shed her clothes and became her other self, her wilder self, were a fantasy? *I could be crazy. Maybe I've only imagined I turn into a cat.*

She'd take fantasy over reality any day. Some days she wondered what it would be like to stay as her other self, to run wild in the woods and never come back. Then it would mean not hearing, "Melanie, is that you, lazy girl? Get over here. I soiled myself. And the bed."

Of course she had, because her mother wouldn't wear a diaper. Too degrading. But apparently shitting herself wasn't.

"Coming, Maizie." She sighed as she set the groceries on the counter. Would this nightmare never end?

That evening, as she laced her mother's cocoa with a sleeping agent, one prescribed by the doctor to give Melanie a break, she decided she needed to get out. To breathe. She'd been cooped up for months now, at her mother's beck and call, only managing to slip away for short periods of time, barely enough to get her paws wet.

Tonight the moon would rise, full and fat. Tonight, while her mother slept, she'd let herself run wild.

Free.

And maybe never come back.

Chapter 3

I should go back. Bryce had been out for a while now, enjoying the brisk evening air. This time of the year everything smelled so crisp.

The moon shone bright overhead, caressing the skin of his back, bathing him in its soft glow. He tossed his head, letting the light catch his rack, the huge antlers casting a shadow on the ground. A crown for the king.

He trotted through the forest, kicking up leaves, avoiding the low-hanging branches. After a day of dealing with his grandfather and the threats, Bryce needed to get out, relax. Stretch his legs and remind himself that his grandfather was being extra ornery of late because of his enforced bed rest. No one liked to be an invalid.

If Bryce could have taken a picture of his evening stroll and sent it to the old bastard, he would have.

Captioned it too. *Wish you were here.* *#walkingtherack*

Grandfather would have flipped. The old man hated not being able to shift and get out of bed, but the doctor said nothing strenuous. The open-heart surgery had taken a lot out of his grandfather. Even though he healed quicker than a human, his age made his health more precarious. Grandfather had gotten a taste of mortality and railed against it.

The sound of the stream beckoned, the thought of crisp water too tempting to resist. He had no fear on his lands. His family owned hundreds of wild acres, free of hunters and prying eyes.

What it didn't prevent was other animals from roaming. As Bryce neared the stream's edge, he froze as the scent of a predator tickled past.

Cat. But not the right smell for the wild cougars rarely seen in this part of Canada. Nor was it a simple housecat or even the larger Maine Coon. What kind was it?

He'd learned at an early age—at the insistence of his grandfather—to identify the varied species' scents. Some kids went to the zoo to ooh and aah over the animals. Bryce went to learn his smells, and usually had to endure a quiz afterwards.

Slowly, he moved out of the cover of trees, not out of any real fear. A big beast like himself didn't fear anything. However, startling something with claws could leave scratches.

At first, he didn't see the feline, crouched low at the water's edge, head ducked and across from him, but a shift of shadows and the glint of its eyes gave away its position.

The tips of its fur were frosted in white, whereas the rest of it was a shade of gray. A tail, edged in black, swished. The feline face lifted, regarding him with golden eyes, the tufts of fur puffing from its cheeks identifying it as a lynx, a rarity, especially in these parts.

Since when do we have one living in these woods? He'd never come across it before. He took a step forward.

The lynx hissed.

Seriously? On my land? He lowered his rack and shook it.

The cat blinked and cocked its head. Probably admiring it. He lifted his head and struck a regal pose.

The feline chuffed. It sounded amused.

He would have narrowed his gaze if his moose face allowed for it. Laughing at his rack. Did this kitty cat not know who it faced? The Great North's fiercest beast, one of the biggest as well. Other animals wished they could have Bryce's rugged countenance. His thick shaggy brown coat. And his legs...he could run over thirty-five miles an hour, over uneven terrain.

The cat yawned and lay down by the water, lazily batting the current. Pretending disinterest. Surely pretending because no one could ignore his grand presence.

Arrogant? Totally. There were not many moose, especially intelligent ones like him, roaming the world. He was a creature to be admired.

The feline rolled on its back, four legs in the air.

Utter disrespect. Bryce dipped his head and wetted the tines of his rack then shook his head, shaking the droplets free. They soaked quite nicely in the lynx's fur.

With a yowl, the cat flipped upright and glared at him. Her back rounded, her hackles rose, and she pulled back a lip.

He turned around and showed his insouciance by kicking up some dirt and striding away. Head held high, he trotted, knowing she admired his rear. Would have walked all the way back to the house except he heard something, a distant howl. Then another in a lower timbre.

Wolves. Not unusual in and of itself. The local pack, which numbered just over twenty in number around town, had permission to use these woods. Most bands of shifters in the area did.

Grandfather might be curmudgeonly in some ways, but when it came to keeping their secret and helping others of his kind, he honored the treaties his great relatives enacted.

The yipping, several of them together, grew louder, and he thought of the cat.

A possible *were* cat. The actions had a certain cognizance behind them.

If any of them are shifters, they'll know the rules and abide by them.

The howls became sharp excited barks, and that was when he heard it. The first yowl.

He stopped walking.

Awoo.

He turned his head to peer behind him.

Don't get involved.

Rawr.

A moose couldn't sigh or he would have as he turned around and began trotting quickly back in the direction from which he'd come. He picked up speed and barreled through the trees, lighter on his feet than most people expected, and fast. He reached the river and took in everything with a quick glance.

The lynx backed against the water's edge, snarling and body arched, trying to make itself look larger. Three wolves faced it, their muzzles pulled to show teeth and growling.

Bryce trumpeted a warning—which the wolves ignored.

He didn't slow his pace as he charged, right at the streaming water, a soaring leap taking him over. His hooves hit the soft bank on the other side, and he stumbled slightly. Righted himself. Reared upward as the closest wolf took aim with its paw.

Is he daring to strike at me?

The claws missed, and Bryce trampled down, managing to strike a good blow.

The wolf yelped and retreated, leaving only two of his mangy companions.

He lowered his head, rack in position to cause serious damage.

The wolves went silent as they turned tail and ran.

He gave chase, galloping after them, cursing mentally as they split apart, forcing him to choose one.

He went left and kept sight of the tail. He wanted to run the wolf down and ask it questions. The oversized dog was a shifter, like him, which meant it recognized that lynx, the female, was also one of them.

It also had to have known who Bryce was. Only one family of moose in the area and everyone knew them.

How dare those mangy curs attack. And on Elanroux land.

The wolf slowed as they hit the graveled edge of a road. The cur began to change, fur receding, limbs shaping, and the man who stood up was slender and dark haired, his pock-marked face distinctive.

Hoof clomping on the hard surface of the road, Bryce took a step towards the fellow who compounded his crimes by giving him the finger. Sudden bright lights from around the bend blinded him but didn't prevent him from realizing his moose versus a big truck wouldn't feel good.

Bryce stumbled back, and the SUV shot past,

slowing only for a moment, long enough for the naked stranger to jump in.

Fuckers. Cursed as they sped away, but retained enough wits to memorize the last four letters of the license plate: BYTU.

With no further pursuit available, he returned to the woods, heading back to the river. No surprise, the lynx was gone, the scent, female and feline, ending at the edge of water. Had the cat gone into the creek to hide its tracks?

Good thinking.

As for him, no point in sticking around. Someone had to be told about this. No matter his issues with his grandfather, this couldn't remain a secret. An attack on their land was an open act of rebellion. A serious crime.

He hurried back to the house—the many acres he'd wandered taking him time. He emerged from the woods shortly after midnight, a man with his shirt untucked, walking barefoot, carrying his shoes. The items were dry because he'd stashed them in a secured weather-tight bin a wee way inside the forest.

Bryce immediately went to his grandfather's room, intent on speaking to him, even if he had to wake the old man, only to pause just outside the door.

He heard voices.

Male voices.

He pushed open the portal and frowned at the guy

standing by his grandfather's bed. A fellow as tall as him, his hair a golden blond, his eyes a vivid blue.

"Who are you?" he barked.

"Say hello to your cousin Rory. And before you start your bitching, I suggest you get nice and close for a whiff of him," Grandfather suggested.

Implying...

Bryce drew near and inhaled. Smelled something canine. Not moose, but definitely a shifter.

"Pleasure to meet you, cousin." Rory held out his hand.

Grabbing it, Bryce stared at the guy as the battle of strength began, the two of them posturing for superiority. Eyeballing each other, chests out, gauging the other's worth.

A clap of hands broke the impasse as Grandfather crowed, "Glad you're both here. Means I just have to say it once. Had the doctor in today for a check-up."

"And?" Bryce asked. "How much longer do you have to stay in bed?"

"A while longer because it's not looking good." Grandfather mustered a suspicious cough. "Doctor says I need to get my affairs in order, which means deciding on an heir."

"What's there to decide?" Bryce growled. "I'm standing right here." He shot a look at the old man, lying in bed, clutching his sheet. He didn't look like a dying man.

"You might be standing here, but I've got my

doubts as to whether you'll do your part to continue the family name."

"Don't you start with the marriage shit again," Bryce groaned.

"Marriage is a wonderful thing. I loved your grandma until the day she left this earth."

"So, why not wait until I fall in love?" Which would happen like never. No woman would ever be interesting enough for him to give up the single life and share his bed. A man liked to sprawl at night.

"I don't have time to wait. I need to know the future is taken care of. So, here's the deal, boys. Whoever gets married first and impregnates his bride is going to be my heir."

"You're fucking senile," spat Bryce. "You can't make this a competition. You don't even know if this guy is related to us."

"I will soon enough, but seriously, look at him. How can you doubt it?" Grandfather pointed.

Bryce refused to look. No denying his supposed cousin had the same brilliant blue gaze. "Appearances mean nothing. I'm your grandson."

"And he's my nephew. The important thing here is making sure my legacy stays in the family."

The fraud cleared his throat. "While I appreciate your warm welcome, uncle. Now is probably time to mention the unfair advantage I have with your stipulation, given I'm already engaged."

"Engaged?" Grandfather pushed himself up in bed. "Excellent. When's the wedding?"

"We haven't chosen a date yet. However, we have spoken of doing it soon. We just need to tidy our schedules. It was a touch unexpected, but I just couldn't resist popping the question." Rory smiled.

Slick. The guy was super slick. Bryce bristled. "That's bullshit. He's lying. He just made up a fiancée because of your contest."

"Don't accuse a man of lying just so you can triumph by default, boy." Grandfather gave him a stern stare. "Be a good sport and win, fair and square."

"You're blackmailing us into getting married."

"I'm asking you to do the right thing," grandfather stated with an implacable stare.

"I, for one, am okay with the stipulations, cousin. But I understand if you're chicken."

No, I'm a moose. I fear nothing...but losing his freedom.

There had to be a way out of this mess. A way to satisfy his grandfather long enough to prove this Rory was an imposter and to make sure he got what he deserved.

But in order to buy time, he might have to find himself a bride—and curtail his freedom.

#betweenarackandahardplace

Chapter 4

I'd do anything to be free. Peel gum from under theatre seats. Bark like a dog on her hands and knees. Heck, she'd even part with part of her soul if she could set herself free of the annoyance of caring for an unappreciative witch. Selfish and unkind didn't even come close to describing Maizie.

Today's rant was how Melanie had caused the cancer. Apparently, by leaving her mother to go to college—best four years of her life—she'd caused Maizie to get sick. The logic went: Melanie left, forcing Maizie to do everything by herself—you know things like her own laundry, cleaning, and, the horror of all horrors, making her own meals. The stress of that led Maizie to drink, which then created the cancer in her liver.

Totally untrue, of course. People were responsible for their own actions. Yet the guilt gnawed at Melanie.

Propositioned by the Billionaire Moose

She tried to ignore it. She truly did. However, it came back, much like her poison ivy rash did if she so much as saw a patch of it.

At times she wondered, had she done something wrong?

No. Hell, no. Melanie didn't deserve this punishment, which was why she scrounged up a dollar and eighty-three cents by going through couch cushions and her purse.

Not enough for a fancy coffee. Barely enough for hot water with coloring, but she knew a place. A place she could buy a cup of something she didn't prepare and enjoy it.

As soon as Melanie entered the knock-off version of a popular chain, she smelled the grinds of coffee and noticed a good-sized crowd. No faces greeted her, just heads bent over laptops and tablets, the tables they'd commandeered meant for only one or two antisocial people. People intent on their own world.

A long counter running along two of the walls put the patrons side by side, and yet they still didn't really peek at each other. In today's society, people kept their heads down, and hid. Hid intentionally even though they didn't have to. These humans with their devices didn't know how lucky they were that they could live freely and openly. Didn't have to hide a feline within that thought she should bat at the man bun of the guy sitting hunched over.

How she envied them. Envied them their simple lives.

The door opened, bringing in with it the sound of the street, busy at this time of the afternoon, and a smell. An odd scent that made her think of the musk of a wild animal that had rolled in a puddle of cologne. She paid it no mind.

She smelled stuff all the time and wondered if it was normal or if she had a heightened olfactory sense. So many things she didn't know about her feline side, and the internet proved more hindrance than help. Old stories and legends spoke of shapeshifters, people who could swap skin for fur. Science claimed it was impossible.

She begged to differ.

The largest source of information she found came surprisingly enough from romance books. A plethora of stories existed with men and women like her, but how to separate fact from fiction? And where were these hunky alpha men who liked to claim their mate?

Meow. Inner kitty was liking the smell of the man behind her. She ignored it. Inner kitty also liked the smell of raw fish.

The body behind brushed closer, invading her space. She thought about telling him to back off but clamped her lips tight. Instead, she shuffled forward and stared at the board, mentally calculating the prices, realizing she had enough for a latte but not a tip. That seemed rude. *I could tip if I got a plain coffee.* But she didn't want a plain coffee, dammit.

She peeked at her clenched fist, mentally willing the coins to double.

"Marry me." The words were distinct enough to startle. Who proposed in the middle of a lineup for burnt, put-hair-on-your-chest coffee? Melanie wanted to know and craned to peek behind her, her view blocked by the impossibly wide chest of the man behind her. A chest that went up, up, up—

Oops. Caught looking by tall, dark, and handsome, who smiled down at Melanie while his blue eyes danced with mirth. She averted her gaze and faced forward again.

"Marry me." Again the words sounded so close. Whoever was asking must have been hiding behind the linebacker-wide body of the guy behind her.

Doesn't look too good, buddy. If you've asked her twice and not gotten a reply, then perhaps you should quit now before things get really embarrassing.

The line shuffled forward, and the big guy behind her bumped into her back. Before she could flash him a look because really, cute or not, respect the space, a rumbled whisper came right by her ear. "Marry me."

Tall, handsome dude was talking to her? Her mouth spoke before she could think. "Are you insane?"

"Only on full moons."

"Bug someone else." What Melanie said. Yet her kitty perked right up. *Turn around.*

Nope.

Next in line for service, she ignored him to step forward and place her order with the barista, only she didn't step forward alone. The big guy stayed close, inside her bubble. Which meant she could smell him.

Smell the thick cologne and a hint of something else…Something—

"What do ya want?" asked the barista, snapping her gum.

"A small black coffee please," Melanie said.

"You're waiting in line for a small coffee?" the big guy said a touch incredulously.

"It is a coffee shop." Counting out her change, Melanie handed over a good chunk of it, and then the rest was dumped in the cardboard cup marked "tips" in black marker.

"In a place like this, you're supposed to get something over the top." He stepped closer, angling his way into the register. "I need a café mocha, heavy on the whipped cream, with a double toasted everything bagel with extra cream cheese, plus a large espresso, no sugar, a half-dozen honey glazed donuts, and a bran muffin."

"A bran muffin?" she couldn't help but mutter.

He heard and tossed her a smile that melted her insides. "Not for me. My grandfather. He'll bitch and moan if he gets nothing."

"Is the espresso to kill him?"

"No, that's for me. The café mocha," said as he

swiped her small cup off the counter before she could and tossed it in a bin, "is for you. As are the donuts."

Who the hell did he think he was? "I don't need you buying me stuff."

"You might not need it, but I'm going to buy it anyhow." He presented the cup with the clear top, showing off the thick whipped cream and the cherry nestled in it.

It did look good.

She shook her head. "I can't accept it."

"You have to. I can't have my future wife saying I cheaped out on our first date."

She blinked. The conversation had veered into psycho territory. "We are not on a date."

"Are you sure? I mean I just bought you breakfast, which we are now going to eat together. Dice it any way you like, but that's a date."

The arrogance of the statement was almost too much. Rather than grabbing the donuts or the upgraded coffee, she turned around and stalked out, murmuring under her breath, "And this is me ditching you on our first date."

Melanie didn't bother to turn around and see his expression. Mr. I-think-I'm-so-hot was probably soothing his bruised ego over having gotten rejected.

Did women seriously fall for this corny marry-me line? Probably, which was why he had perfected his stalking by following her outside.

"You should have said you preferred to eat and walk. I love *exercise*."

The inflection had her whirling to glare. "This is harassment." What she said. Yet her inner kitty seemed to think, *This is fun!*

"I would have said this was more friendly banter. Just getting to know my lovely bride-to-be."

"Are you off your meds? On drugs? Hallucinating? Because I have no interest in you."

He smiled, and she couldn't help but think what a shame he was obviously a few cards short of a full deck. The man was stupidly handsome.

"Nothing wrong with me. And you are perfect."

"Me, perfect?" The casual compliment shouldn't have caused her heart rate to speed up.

"More than perfect, given I need a wife, a certain kind of wife, and you need"—he paused—"something."

Pride straightened her. "Is this your way of remarking on the fact I look like a poor hag?"

"More like a shabby rose in need of some TLC. Let me give you that care."

She gaped. "Did you just proposition me?"

"Yes. No. I mean, yes, because I am not joking when I claim I need to get married."

"Need?"

"Yes need, and quickly too."

The entire conversation had a surreal feel to it. "So you're just proposing to strangers out of the blue?"

"Not exactly. You're the first person I've asked.

Hopefully the last. Just say yes, would you? I don't have time to be picky. He's already ahead of me."

"Who is?

"Rory. My so-called cousin."

The name meant nothing. "What does your cousin have to do with me?"

He sighed. "It's complicated."

"You think?" A bit of sarcasm in there.

"I promise I'll explain in greater detail, but the short version is Rory's the reason I need to get married. Actually my grandfather is the one who started this nonsense. See, he's dying, and he wants me married before he goes."

"Sure he does." She crossed her arms over her chest and sneered. "Let me guess, he's worth millions."

"Billions."

At that, she made a noise.

"It's true."

"Do I really look that dumb?" That kind of scenario happened only in movies and books.

"It's the truth. Which is why I'm proposing a marriage of convenience with a few extra *perks*." The sensual tilt of lips again alluded to a more sensual pursuit.

It gave her a little tingle. She ignored it. She'd not remained chaste through college by falling for pretty smiles. Her mother might not have taught her much growing up, but she had taught her not to spread her legs. The yelled, *Don't be a whore,* every time she walked out helped.

"If this is how you get girls into bed, it's pretty slimy."

"This isn't a game."

"Really? Then tell me how your grandfather became a billionaire. Did he invest in diamonds? Oil?"

"Maple syrup." He said it so seriously. So proudly.

Melanie couldn't help but snicker.

Chapter 5

THE WOMAN LAUGHED. FULLY AND COMPLETELY. And he could only stare.

Her almost silver hair, grayish in hue yet not with age, glinted in the sun, the darker weaving strands almost striping it, the tips frosted white. Even in this shape, she kept her yellow cat eyes, the glow of them brilliant and almost disconcerting.

By chance, he'd found the lynx from the forest. Caught her scent as he passed by on the sidewalk, intent on his favorite bakery.

What's that? It caught his attention, teased him with ghostly scented fingers urging him to follow it inside. He'd known her immediately, even though she faced away. Her appearance distinct. Her scent, remarkable and completely unhidden.

He couldn't resist. Couldn't help but see her as the solution to his problem. It wasn't hard to tell she needed help. Needed money. Her clothes looked well worn, the jacket frayed at the hems, her shoes gray with wear, not by design. Then the final proof, the assortment of change she used to buy the cheapest thing in the place.

This woman probably barely owned more than what was on her back and yet she dared laugh at his heritage.

"You have a problem with maple syrup?"

"It's that stuff made from trees, isn't it? Or do you offer the knock-off kind made of brown sugar?"

He drew himself upright. "There is only one true kind of maple syrup, and my family has been making it for generations." Liquid gold in his world. Their premium line fetched the highest prices on the market.

"Well, la-dee-da for you. I don't eat the stuff. Too sweet." Her nose wrinkled, adorably cute, and yet the blasphemy in her words had him exclaiming.

"Too sweet? Never. It's a matter of using it to complement in the right amount with other foods."

"You eat it with pancakes."

"Not just pancakes. French toast, waffles, drizzled over a salty ham. Basted over a chicken breast on the barbecue."

Again, her soft laughter tickled. "You are way too excited about syrup."

"Because it's delicious. You'll learn to love it once we're married."

She snorted. "I think you've been sniffing too much maple, big guy."

"The name is Bryce."

"Don't care."

"You should, Ms..."

"None of your business."

"That's not very friendly. What's your name?" When he saw her hesitate, he cajoled. "Come on, it won't hurt to tell me."

A sigh escaped her. "Melanie."

Nice. Classic. Grandfather would approve. "I'm surprised we've never met." He thought he knew all the shifters in town.

"I only moved in recently with my mother."

"And you didn't register?"

"Register what?" Her brow creased. "To vote? Is there an election?"

"No." He cocked his head. "But you should have presented yourself to my grandfather. We'll take care of that when we tell him we're engaged."

"Not engaged, dude. And I don't understand why you keep persisting. You claim you're rich, so why marry me? Why not some rich girl you've known all your life?"

"Because she won't want to leave once she's not needed." Bryce had figured it out since his grandfather had made the ultimatum. He only had to make the pretense of complying with his grandfather. Soon, they'd find out Rory wasn't part of the family and his granddad would change his will to make Bryce the only heir.

"So you want a sham wife who'll walk away." She snorted. "Why would anyone agree to that?"

He cast her a glance. "Money."

"I'm not for sale."

She whirled and began to walk away. He grabbed her arm, and a jolt of awareness hit. He noted the thin leanness of the limb, yet the wiry strength underneath.

"Let me go." She tugged.

"At least say you'll think about it. A fake engagement, worst-case scenario, a marriage in name only for a few months."

"Still not interested." She pulled free. "Good luck convincing someone of your story." She walked away, a slim figure in a jean jacket, her loose hair lifting in the wind.

A true natural beauty, and a shifter. Dress her up in a slim pencil skirt and jacket and granddad would gobble her up.

If she agreed.

He frowned because she didn't seem inclined. She'd also forgotten to give him her phone number.

Good thing being rich had its advantages.

I'll convince you to become my fake bride, little kitty. He just needed the right kind of incentive.

Chapter 6

Entering the apartment, Melanie felt her mood sink. Despite the sunshine outside, it was dark inside, the blinds all drawn tight. The lights turned off. They could barely afford to keep anything on. The bill was overdue, and it was only a matter of time before they shut off the power, again.

The shuttered windows made the whole place stuffy. The stench of sickness suffocated. After the fresh crisp air of the fall outside, it hit her like a slap. Reminded her she was no better than a prisoner allowed only small respites.

Actually, today Melanie didn't get a treat. She'd never gotten her coffee because that crazy guy tossed it, and in her pride, she'd not snared the whipped cream replacement.

With a cherry.

How decadent.

"Where have you been, lazy girl?" The harangue began, the words barking out of the bedroom, and Melanie did her best not to flinch. While she knew the words were meant to hurt, it didn't make it any easier, and she couldn't seem to completely ignore them.

"Melanie!" Maizie shrieked. "I want out of this bed."

And so her day went. Caring for an ungrateful woman. Nothing to brighten her day except for her encounter with that man.

The maple syrup mogul. Snicker. Surely he lied.

When her mother went to bed, she dug out her phone. Not a recent model. Nothing as fancy as that, and the screen was cracked, hence her deal on it, but it could get on the internet. The Wi-Fi from the fast food place across the street might prove slow, but it worked.

She did a search. Towering Oaks, the name of the town, and maple syrup.

Thousands of pings, most of them for the Elanroux factory, the biggest one of what she read were dozens across the country. Family owned according to the history. Would the stranger's picture be in the company directory?

She looked, unable to stem her curiosity. Surely he lied.

I'll be damned.

There he was, Bryce Theodore Elanroux. She

stared at his image, a bit more serious than she'd seen him, his haircut fresh and short, his tie perfectly straight.

No mistaking him. The man who'd proposed to her.

He had to be kidding. Pulling the leg of the poor girl. Offering up a sob story of a dying granddad to get in her pants most likely. Except hadn't she seen an article recently with the name Elanroux in it?

She searched again and soon was reading all about it.

Theodore Maven Elanroux, a distinguished member of our community and great-grandson of an original founding father, has fallen gravely ill. Sources claim there is much uncertainty about his recovery. He is succeeded by his grandson, Bryce, born of his now departed daughter, Kelly.

Most of the articles had the same things to say, how Theo took over from his dad and then took in his grandson to teach him the family business. Nothing linking Bryce or his granddad to any scandals. No rumors of impending nuptials.

Only one little paragraph hinted at something in this week's online edition of the local news.

It was with great joy that Theodore Elanroux was reunited with his nephew, Rory Beauchamp. A source close to Rory says the family is pulling together in this time of need. With Rory stating, "While overjoyed with this reunion, we are saddened by my uncle's poor health. My fiancée and I just hope we can throw together the wedding before anything happens."

So part of the story Bryce had told her was true. But surely the whole needing to get married part wasn't.

Wiggling on the couch to get comfy—a couch that doubled as a bed—she couldn't help but wonder if he'd meant it. Maybe Bryce truly did want to get married to make a dying old man happy.

Kind of sweet. Which didn't excuse his methods.

Bzzt. Bzzt. Her phone vibrated in her hand, shaking like an angry bee. She kept the ringer off lest it annoy her mother. The last time Maizie heard the phone, she'd gotten her hands on it and tossed it, narrowly missing the sink full of sudsy water. She claimed Melanie didn't need outside distractions.

Wrong. She needed any distraction she could get.

Since Melanie didn't recognize the number, she let it ring through. Only a few friends from college had this number and most had stopped calling weeks ago. No one wanted to talk to a depressed girl. Probably a telemarketer.

Bzzt. Bzzt. It rang again, same number. It roused her curiosity. She clicked the green phone button. "Hello?"

"Did you think on it?"

"Who is this?" she asked despite knowing—had

guessed, foolishly hoped—from the moment her heart leaped at the first ring.

"Don't play dumb. You know who this is. Did you think about my proposal?"

"How did you get my number?"

"I'm rich. It's not that hard."

"If you're so rich, then why not rent a model to pretend to be your fiancée?" Because surely that would make things easier.

"I would if I found one who fit the requirement."

"And what requirement is that? Lack of mental capacity? No way you're serious about engaging in a platonic marriage with financial benefits." He was a guy. Guys always wanted sex.

"I'm not an animal in that respect. I can restrain myself. Can you?"

The turnabout caught her off guard. "Excuse me?"

"I asked if you would have a problem keeping your hands off me. Not that I'd mind, you are quite attractive. But keep in mind, this is a business proposition, so if you touch, it doesn't mean we'll stay married."

If she touched? "This is crazy. I'm not touching you, or marrying you. I don't even know why I'm talking to you."

"Because you're intrigued. This is exciting stuff, and you can't help but wonder, what would it be like? Imagine waking every day in a mansion, your every need catered to."

Sounded decadent. But impossible. "I can't go anywhere; my mother is sick. She needs me."

"That's where money can help. I could hire you a nurse. Two, even, to provide round-the-clock care."

"That's super expensive."

"And? That is only one of the perks. Once we married, you wouldn't have to work at all unless you wanted to."

"Not work, so I can be dependent on you, the big man, for funds." She rolled her eyes even if he couldn't see her expression.

"You misunderstand. As my future bride, you'll have access to family assets for all your needs. And you wouldn't need permission from me to withdraw them."

Unlimited resources... She shook her head. "Are you seriously resorting to bribery?"

"Think of it as a financial promise. You do me a favor. I do you a favor."

"Pretty big favors."

"What do you have to lose?"

Self-respect? Then again, she didn't really have any or she'd never let her mother abuse her like she did.

"Melanie!" The screech arrived loud and clear. "I need my pain meds. Where are you, lazy girl? What did I do to deserve such a cow of a daughter?"

She closed her eyes and held in a sigh. "I have to go."

"Help me and I'll help you."

He made it sound so easy. She hung up.

That night as mother screamed, demanding her services for the fifth time, leaving Melanie exhausted and bleary-eyed, she wondered if it truly could be real. Could she accept the billionaire's proposition?

Only one way to find out.

Chapter 7

His secretary rang. "Sir, there is a woman here to see you."

"Really?" Bryce brightened for a moment—*she's gonna say yes!*—only to deflate as Chanice entered. With her came the smell of wolf. Someone had been hanging with her pack before coming over here.

"Darling, it's been ages." She used such arrogant airs, and yet Chanice was younger than him at twenty-four. Twenty-four and angling for a husband. Grandfather would be more than happy if he settled down with her.

But Bryce somehow doubted she'd agree to anything fake. Chanice was all about advancement and social status. She'd make a perfect trophy wife, but he could easily see her eventually becoming a widow. Whereas Bryce would prefer to live to a ripe old age, which meant he'd stay far away from the woman.

Of course, he thought that now. As a teen, he'd been more than happy to take what she offered.

"I didn't know you were back in town," he remarked.

She waved a hand, showing off her manicure, a sharp contrast to the woman he'd met with her nails cut to the quick. "I was, but my fiancé"—and, yes, she made sure to flash the ring—"had some family stuff to attend to. So I joined him."

"Congrats on getting engaged." He wondered what poor SOB in her pack had gotten stuck with her. Must be one of the richer ones because she wouldn't settle for anything less than loaded.

"Yes, I'm quite excited about it."

"Do I know the lucky guy?"

"You've met him, I think, but enough about me."

He almost retorted, Since when? "What do you want?"

"How have you been? Still single I see?" Her peek at his hand was less than subtle.

"Hopefully not for long."

"Oh. You've met someone?" No mistaking the narrowing of her gaze and the lower tone of her voice.

"Yes."

"Who?" Forget any attempt to sound nice. She almost barked the word.

"I can't say. She's kind of shy." And not interested, yet. But he planned to work on that.

"Well, that's just lovely." Which, given the inflection, sounded more like, *you prick*.

So, of course, he just had to keep needling. "Great girl. Cares for her ailing mother. Just graduated college." But never got a decent full-time job. She went straight home and, according to his research thus far, rarely left it.

"Sounds wonderful." Spoken through gritted teeth.

"She is, but I doubt hearing about my love life is why you're here."

"Can't an old friend pop in to say hello?"

He spoke bluntly. "You never have before."

"You never used to be so boorish either." She stood. "I should go. I am meeting my fiancé for lunch."

"Give him my regards." Also give the man Bryce's thanks for saving mankind from her clutches.

Once Chanice left, he tried to work but found it hard to concentrate. He'd chosen to ensconce himself at the corporate downtown offices today rather than at the factory, wanting to make himself accessible in case *she* came looking. Foolish really. His kitten had seemed rather adamant on the phone.

Yet...he couldn't help but believe she was softening and as intrigued as he was.

So intrigued Bryce had done something he'd never thought he'd do. He'd stalked a woman under the guise of reconnaissance. He'd discreetly shadowed Melanie home the day before, the only way of finding out where she worked or lived. Only then did he manage to set his secretary on a background search.

What he discovered deepened the mystery. First, Melanie Rusch wasn't a native of Towering Oaks. Her mother had moved here about three years ago—a year after her daughter left for college, and Maizie got booted for non-payment of rent.

Since arriving in Towering Oaks, Maizie Rusch had been evicted from two more properties and would have added a third to that if she hadn't fallen ill.

Which was where Melanie came in. She'd been in town several months now. She'd worked a few part-time jobs, but discreet inquiries as to why they didn't last long resulted in one simple answer: The mother.

Mother Rusch constantly called and harassed, making it impossible for Melanie to do her job.

What a prize.

His digging also revealed Melanie was single, with no social media to speak of, although he did manage to find a picture of her at college, smiling happily during exam week, a kitten in her lap as part of the college's de-stressing programs.

His obsession with her was a tad crazy. He could argue all he wanted that she was perfect for the sham, yet, the more he dug, the more curious he found himself about the woman—and the cat.

How had she come by her lynx side? He'd have to meet the mother in person to be sure, but he'd wager it wasn't her since the woman had never presented herself upon arriving in town, which was in clear defiance of the rules all shifters abided by.

Which left the missing father. A man not named on paper. Not even on the birth record he'd managed to have dug up.

Unknown.

What man left behind his child?

I'd never do it. Bryce might be many things, including an arrogant liar who was determined to pull the wool over his grandfather's eyes, but he did take his responsibilities seriously. So seriously he was prepared to marry a stranger.

A woman he felt compelled to see, which was why he told his secretary he had to leave early.

Exiting the building, he paused. He couldn't have said why except something nagged him. Tugged him into turning. He spotted her across the street, chin tilted upwards, staring at the office building, chewing her lower lip.

Only one reason for her to be here.

Me.

He strode across the street, confidence oozing and stopping traffic. Melanie caught sight of him halfway, and he could see by her startled expression she thought about running.

She came close.

Then her shoulders straightened, and he could almost see resolve pouring from her.

"Hello," he said, coming to a stop in front of her,

hands shoved in his pockets. "Did you come to see me?"

"No."

"Are you really going to lie?"

She sighed. "Fine. You caught me. I came to see you."

"Did you make a decision?"

Even the thought of it had him tingling, and he might have let out an exuberant whoop when she announced, "I'll become your fake wife."

Chapter 8

She'd done it. Agreed to marry a virtual stranger on the promise he'd make her life worth living again.

And what did he do? Said, "Excellent. I'll have a lawyer friend draw up the terms of our agreement."

Probably the most unromantic thing she'd ever heard, and yet, what did she expect? He never claimed to propose out of love. Which suited her fine. This would be a business arrangement, pure and simple. The fact that seeing him made her pulse race and her blood run hot meant nothing. Nothing except she obviously needed to get out more, because she shouldn't find herself attracted to a pompous rich boy who'd, in essence, bought her services, and the first thing expected of her was dinner tonight at his home with his family.

Over fancy coffee—which Bryce paid for—at a

posh little café with intimate booths, he'd given her a brief outline of his expectations.

Dress nice. Be polite. Pretend affection for him. Go along with anything he said.

"Should I walk behind you three paces, too?" she couldn't help but drawl when he took a breath.

"Only if you're admiring my ass," he'd replied, making her blush.

As to a backstory. They would stick to the facts with a twist. They met in a coffee shop and were smitten. The engagement would come in a few days.

"Isn't that too soon?" Melanie queried.

"Not if we were smitten at first sight."

She snorted. "No one will believe that of you."

"They will if we play our parts right. We just have to be careful we don't come across too fake."

"Gee, more fake than you proposing to a stranger?" She blew a raspberry before taking a sip of an espresso that had enough caffeine to keep her awake into next week.

"Some of the best love stories have started with a chance encounter."

Except they weren't in love.

"What if someone calls us out?"

"And says what?" he asked with an arch of his brow. "My grandfather told me to get married. Given he knows I'm not seeing anyone seriously, your sudden appearance won't bother him at all."

"What if he hates me?"

At that, Bryce laughed. "I wouldn't worry about that. One sniff and he is going to love you."

Sniff? Weird family. She hoped his granddad liked the smell of baby powder deodorant because she didn't own any perfume.

Nor did she possess clothes that would suit a fancy dinner for that matter. Not that she said anything to Bryce. Just because she'd agreed to the deal didn't mean she'd start begging. Heck, she still had no idea what kind of benefit she'd get out of it. So far, she'd gotten good coffee and a chance to feel giddy. Excited. Hot.

Her inner feline wanted to purr and rub herself all over the man. Had he bathed in catnip?

Despite the fact this was purely business, he managed to make her laugh and smile. A smile that waned once he dropped her off, because he insisted on taking her home.

Not only had he shown tenacity in hunting down her phone number, he knew where she lived. He fit the definition of a stalker. Oddly enough, it felt more endearing than frightening, which might explain why so few women called the cops when good-looking men did it.

Only as Bryce left did he remind her he'd be picking her up at six. Leaving her two hours to not look dirt poor and terrified.

Having spent too much time away, she wasn't surprised to hear mother bellowing the moment she walked in the door. "Where have you been? Ungrateful chit."

So ungrateful, Melanie might have bargained her soul to dig them out of the pit they were in.

"I was running errands," she said as she dropped her purse on the scarred coffee table.

"What did you bring me?"

A loaded syringe? Only in her dreams. She carried the Styrofoam container with her leftovers into the room.

"What's that?" Maizie's blood-shot eyes, tinged in yellow, narrowed in suspicion. "Did you steal from me to buy it?"

"I didn't steal. I saw a friend while in town, and they took me for coffee. I brought you a treat."

"Friend, what friend?" Mother snapped. "You have no friends. Because you're pathetic." Said the woman who'd yet to get a single visit or phone call.

"Do you want it or not?" Melanie asked, holding out the container with the frosted Danish.

"No." Maizie slapped her hand, sending the box flying. Then began to harangue.

Shutting her ears to it, Melanie left the room, but she could still hear it. All the reasons why she was a failure.

Mother was still loudly complaining when she went to answer a firm knock at the door. While hoping for a man in a robe with a scythe, she instead confronted a thickset woman with a kind face wearing scrubs patterned with cartoons.

Melanie scrunched her nose, especially since her inner kitty hissed and seemed to think the mild-looking woman in front of her was a threat. "Um, can I help you?"

"Miss Rusch I presume. I'm Martha. Mr. Elanroux sent me."

"Sent you?" Struck a little dumb, it took her a moment of staring at the stethoscope around the woman's neck to feel a faint prick of hope.

"Apparently you're in need of a companion for your mother. One with medical training."

Melanie could still hear the bitching from the bedroom and stepped into the hall, shutting the door. "I don't know if you want to do this. My mother can be"—a cunt, a mean vindictive bitch—"difficult."

The nurse reached out to grab her hands. "Don't you worry, little sweetie. I've handled bigger grumbly bears than her. Mr. Elanroux sent me to help, and by the sounds of it, you could use a break. I hear you've got a date."

"Yes, but—" She cast a glance over her shoulder at the door.

The hands around hers squeezed. "No buts. Why don't you go get ready? I'll handle your mother."

Martha seemed determined, so why did Melanie argue? Wasn't this why she'd made the deal with Bryce in the first place?

Swinging open the door, Melanie stepped inside before she pointed. "She's in there."

Martha smiled as she swept past, the scent of her clean, with a hint of something woodsy. "Don't you worry that pretty little head of yours."

Don't worry. That was all Melanie did. Yet, she didn't move as Martha entered her mother's room. She listened.

"Who are you?"

"Hello, Mrs. Rusch. I'm Martha, a home care specialist."

"I don't need no home care shit. Get out of my room."

"I can't leave, Mrs. Rusch. I'm here to give your daughter a hand."

"Did that lazy cow hire you? I knew she was stealing from me."

"Your daughter is a lovely young lady. You shouldn't be calling her names. A mama should be proud of her cub. Now what do you say we get some fresh air and light in here."

"Don't touch that curtain. Get out. You're fired."

"You can't fire me. Now sit still so I can take your temperature with my ear thermometer."

"No." Crash.

Melanie winced.

"Well, that wasn't very nice." The nurse remained firm. "Now we'll have to do a rectal reading."

Melanie might have listened longer to the soap opera except there was another knock at the door.

Now what?

Bemused, she answered it and immediately had a package thrust at her. "Delivery for Ms. Rusch."

No signature required meant the guy trotted off down the hall. She slammed the door shut and looked at the box, embossed with the name of a chic boutique. Not a place she could ever shop at.

Inside...

"Oh my." From undergarments to an outfit that probably cost more than her last few paychecks combined.

He'd thought of everything.

If she were a girl who believed in fairy tales, she'd have felt like a princess, which meant it was important to remind herself that he was more like the fairy godmother. Giving her all the tools she needed to feel like a princess, but once midnight hit, and he didn't need her anymore, she'd go back to being an impoverished Cinderella.

But while it lasted, she planned to dance.

When Bryce arrived at six on the nose, she was ready. The outfit—a slim-fitting skirt that hit just past her knees, and a soft sweater—was elegant yet casual. So she'd opted for the same with her hair. Washing and drying it then brushing it until it crackled. A hairclip held it out of her face but left most of it loose. Her makeup was minimal, mostly because she didn't own much other than eyeliner, mascara, and lip-gloss.

As for shoes, the ones he'd sent were thankfully low heeled and, while a bit big, wearable.

She found herself ready far too soon, which meant she had time to panic and regret her decision. Then she'd listened to Martha strong-arm her mother into the shower then into eating her dinner and couldn't help but think, "This is nice." Nice that she wasn't the one playing unpaid nursemaid.

Also nice was the fact she was going out.

I am going on a date. With a man. Even if it was fake, it was the most exciting thing to happen to her in a while.

She swung open the door a scant second after his first brisk knock. Her heart hammered in her chest, and she found herself tongue-tied, mostly because he looked ridiculously good. Wearing slacks and a beige sweater that complemented her baby blue one, he looked casual yet delicious.

We should have a lick. Her inner kitty knew what it wanted to do, especially since he smelled like vanilla —and something else.

There she was thinking there was something familiar about his scent. Something kind of untamed and wild, that made her think of the forest.

"You look stunning," he declared as he thrust a bouquet of flowers at her.

She blinked. "Um, you didn't have to do that."

"How would it look if I arrived for our date empty-handed?"

"But no one is watching."

"Don't kid yourself. Someone is always watching."

"Is that Brycie I hear?" An excited Martha exited the bedroom and beamed at Bryce. "There's the handsome boy." She enveloped him in a bear hug that almost lifted him off his feet.

She mouthed, *Brycie?*

He offered her a sheepish grin over Martha's shoulder. "I see you've met, Martha. She lived with us for a while when my mom was sick."

"Five years," Martha expanded. "And I got to know this cheeky monkey. How is your old coot of a grandfather? I hear he's not feeling so good."

"Recovering, but slowly. I wanted to bring you back to care for him but—"

Martha interrupted. "Let me guess, he didn't want a woman washing his manly parts."

A grin pulled at his lips. "He hasn't changed much."

"But you have," she said. "You've lost weight since I last saw you." Martha patted his stomach. "Are you working too hard again?"

He shrugged. "No more than usual.

"You better teach this boy to relax." Martha turned her gaze on Melanie. "But what am I doing, yapping your ear off. You two run along and have fun. And don't you worry about your mama. I've got it handled."

Propositioned by the Billionaire Moose

For a moment, Melanie debated introducing Bryce to Maizie then thought better of it. No good would come of it.

They left her apartment and took the stairs because the elevator was on the fritz again. They didn't say much until they hit the pavement outside.

"Thank you," she said softly. "For the clothes. The help."

"That's just the start, kitten."

She blinked at the nickname. Surely a coincidence. "Martha seems competent, and nice."

"She is, but unfortunately, she is only temporary," he said. "On such short notice she was the only one who could come. But good news, I've got a new nurse coming in the morning. She, along with two others, will work on rotating shifts to care for your mom."

"All the time?"

"I got the impression your mother needed it."

"She does, but…" What of her privacy? Bad enough she slept on the couch, how would having a third person constantly around work?

"I see the gears in your head whirring. Talk to me," he ordered.

Did he seriously think she'd spill her thoughts because he asked? "It's just so extravagant. I can do some of the work, too, you know."

"So what do you want?"

She shrugged, mostly because she didn't know.

People didn't usually ask. Mother usually screamed. "Maybe a few hours each day for myself."

He frowned. "That doesn't seem like enough. And you'll need to make time for me in the evening if we're going to make this believable."

"Just how believable do you think we can be? We just met."

"Well, for starters, it would help if you didn't shy away every time I got near."

"I don't shy—" He moved close to her, and she took a step away.

"See what I mean? Do I scare you?"

"Yes." She blurted out the word before she could stop it. "It's just you're so..."

"Awesome. Magnificent. Virile."

"Overwhelming. Like a bull rushing in, bowling me over and not giving me a chance to catch my breath."

His lips quirked. "Shouldn't a woman in love be breathless?"

She tossed him a side eye. "Except we're not in love, and at times, you're too much. Like the whole nurse thing. I appreciate it, really I do, but would it have killed you to consult me rather than making all the decisions yourself?"

"But then you would have said no, or second-guessed it, and it was just better if I did it for you."

Which funny enough was exactly what she'd

Propositioned by the Billionaire Moose

wanted a few days ago, and yet now she argued against it. "I'd like a say in the things that affect me."

"If you insist."

"I do insist, or this charade isn't going to work long." She paused beside the car door he opened.

"You need to relax."

"I am relaxed."

"Really?"

She didn't expect him to lunge and grab her around the waist, his hands spanning it, pulling her against his larger frame.

The move startled and her breath caught. She tilted her face to see him staring down at her. "What are you doing?"

"You are like a skittish kitten around me."

He had no idea how true that was. Meanwhile her inner kitty was practically swooning in excitement. It wanted her to get closer. To rub her scent all over him. To lick him...

She tried to draw away, but he held her firmly. "I'm not used to people touching me." Maizie didn't believe in affection or hugs. The only time her mother touched was to give a cuff on the back of the head to move faster.

"Better get used to it because I intend to touch you a lot." He pulled her closer, and her pulse went into overdrive, thumping madly. Blood rushed, making her hear only a roaring rush, and her lips parted.

"That's better. Now you look like a woman waiting for a kiss."

He released her and walked away. Meanwhile she wanted to cry out in disappointment because, dammit, she had been expecting a kiss!

And the jerk didn't give her one. Sad meow.

Chapter 9

IF THE MOMENT HAD A HASHTAG IT WAS PROBABLY #blueballed.

The drive to his house was hard—almost as hard as his erection because, dammit, Melanie looked tempting. So very, very tempting.

In her worn clothes, she'd been attractive. Dress her in something a little more upscale, toss on a light dab of makeup, and with her hair pulled back and shining...wow.

Like big fucking wow. As in, he wanted to toss her over a shoulder, take her somewhere private, and show her how hot he found her wow.

Somehow he doubted she'd agree to that. The only reason she sat in this car was because of the deal they'd made. The realization kept him in check—and his hands on the wheel instead of stroking her thigh.

"Where are we going?" She broke the tense silence in the car.

"The mansion for a family dinner."

"I thought your grandfather was sick."

"He is."

"Yet we're having dinner with him?"

"Yeah. Him, my so-called cousin, his fiancée, and us." His lips twisted into a sneer. "Granddad insisted so we could get to know each other better."

"You don't believe he's your cousin."

"Nope." He popped the 'p' on the answer. "I find it a tad too convenient that, as my grandfather is ailing, some guy we never even suspected existed shows up out of nowhere claiming he's family."

"And your grandfather believed him?"

"So he claims. He is, however, getting a DNA test done. The results are just taking longer than expected."

"I thought DNA stuff was pretty quick these days."

"Usually it is. However, our usual lab had some technical problems, and since we don't trust anyone else"—because they certainly couldn't give shifter blood samples to humans to play with— "we kind of have to wait."

"If I were a believer in conspiracies, I'd say that's very convenient for your cousin."

He slapped the steering wheel and exclaimed, "That's exactly what I said! But grandfather is being a senile old coot. Waxing all sentimental about how Rory looks just like Trixie, if his sister were a girl, of course."

Propositioned by the Billionaire Moose

"What if he really is your cousin?"

His grip tightened on the wheel, making it creak. "He's not."

"But what if he is?" she insisted.

"Then I guess we'd better make sure we're wed before he is." What he didn't add was the pregnant part. Hopefully it wouldn't come to that, although—he cast Melanie a glance—bedding Melanie wouldn't be a hardship. Not one bit.

"Tell me some stuff about yourself. If we're going to make this work, then I should have some kind of idea who you are."

Good point. "I'm twenty-six. I work for Towering Oaks Incorporated. My parents are dead. Dad was shot by a hunter when I was ten." Bloody poacher thought he'd tagged a real moose. Imagine his surprise when he went to bag his prize and found a bleeding man instead. "My mom was taken by a car accident." An event that crushed not only a young boy who loved his mother, but the man who'd sired her. In their grief they'd bonded, but that bond was tested over and over again due to his grandfather's ornery nature. "What about you?"

"You know about my mom. Dying of liver cancer and making everyone suffer along with her." Melanie didn't hide the bitterness in her words. "Never knew my dad. He took off when I was young, too young to remember him. I don't even have a name or a face. My mother never shared anything about him."

"That sucks." At least he'd had time with his.

"Yeah, well, if he didn't care enough to stick around, then it was probably for the best. I don't have much else interesting to add. I went to college. Had just graduated when my mother insisted I care for her."

"No offense, but it doesn't sound as if you like her much."

"I don't."

"Then why did you come back to care for her?"

A deep sigh heaved out of her. "A feeling of obligation. The woman gave birth to me. Then abused me. And heaped guilt upon guilt. Rationally, I know I should walk away..."

"But?" he prodded.

"She's the only family I have. Once she's gone, I'll truly be alone."

The lonely words struck him, especially since he understood. As much as his grandfather drove him batty, he also was his only family tie. Once he died, it would be just Bryce.

Just me. For a moment he understood his grandfather's burning desire to see a great-grandchild. To know that a part of him would live on.

Melanie spoke. "How much of my real life did you want me to use? It's not very glamorous, so I'll understand if you want me to pretend to be someone else."

"No. I want you to be yourself." The world was already full of pretense.

"You do realize that it's not just my upbringing that

will set me apart. I never learned any fancy manners. I might not know which fork to use."

"So long as you don't eat with your hands behind your back, face first in the plate, you'll be fine."

"I think I can manage that." A snicker left her, the mirth-filled sound wrapping around him and tugging forth a smile.

"You'll do great." Better than great because Melanie had an innate sweetness about her, a softness with a steel core. She wouldn't bend easily, but she could be shaped into something wonderful. Someone perfect for a billionaire in need of a wife.

Pulling up in front of the house, behind a sports car with the top down, the vanity plate reading RoryBeau, he paused for a moment.

Could he truly go through this charade? Lie to his grandfather just to inherit?

He looked over at Melanie, biting her lower lip, looking adorable, and it struck him.

Maybe it doesn't have to be fake.

Chapter 10

It wasn't just butterflies dancing in her tummy. Melanie had a few frogs hopping around, an octopus squeezing her innards, plus a pacing nervous kitty making her heart race.

She stood outside a mansion. As in three stories tall, bigger than her apartment building, freaking mansion.

And Bryce lived in it.

He came around the car, frowning. Probably because he'd realized how preposterous her being here was. She didn't fit into this world. She was a fraud.

"You should have waited for me."

"To what?" she asked with a creased brow.

"Open your door and help you out."

She blinked. "But I know how to get out of a car. Why would I need your help?"

"Because it's what gentlemen do."

At that, she laughed. "You mean treat women like invalids?"

"It's called courtesy."

Mischievousness had her popping back into the car and slamming the door shut. He crouched down and peered at her through the window.

"What are you doing?"

"Letting you be a gentleman."

At that, he snorted, but he did open the door and offer his hand. She slid hers into it, and tingling awareness raced through her as he tugged her out.

He didn't release it, even once she stood beside him. She tilted her face to peek at him. "Is that better?" she asked, her voice suddenly husky.

"Much better," he rumbled, his thumb stroking over the skin of her hand.

He held it as he began to move toward the massive front door. She had no choice but to follow. The steps, made of individual stone and not concrete, spanned at least ten feet wide, offering a wide stoop to enter the house.

The portal opened before they reached it, and she bit her tongue lest she giggle, for there, in a suit, looking every inch a butler, was a butler.

"I swear, if you say his name is Alfred, I'm going to start looking for your cape," she muttered.

"The cape would clash with my rack."

An odd statement to make.

"Evening, Kendrick."

"Master Bryce." The butler nodded his head. "If you'll follow me. The other guests have arrived and are seated in the dining room."

"Including grandfather?" Bryce sounded surprised.

"He insisted, sir."

"He's being an idiot," Bryce muttered. "The doctor said he was supposed to preserve his strength. Dinner was supposed to be in his room."

As he pulled Melanie inside, she had only a moment to take in their surroundings. Lots of wood being the predominant theme. Gleaming wood floors, their dark sheen polished and broken up by intricate lighter inlays. The baseboards and door trims were wide and of the same deep color, contrasting with the pale gray walls.

The furniture all appeared antique, the legs spindly, probably hand carved and expensive. Nothing like her melamine furniture at home.

The long hall had several doors along it, pocket ones that provided a grand entrance when Kendrick grabbed the handles and slid them into the wall recess.

She wanted to hide and most definitely blushed hot when Kendrick, in a most somber tone, announced, "Master Bryce and his lady friend, Melanie Rusch."

How had the butler known her name when they'd not been introduced, she wondered?

It took a moment of ogling the giant dining space—walls papered in burgundy and gold leaf, the wainscoting the same dark wood as the floor. The massive table stretched long enough to feed a football team, the chairs lined in two rows with a more massive throne-like one at each end.

Candelabra lit the room, the candles providing flickering light, enough of them that she could see the occupants. A young man with blond hair, a gorgeous woman with the brightest red lipstick she'd ever seen, and an older fellow, tucked into some blankets at the head of the table.

"There you are, my boy. I was beginning to wonder if you'd join us."

"Wouldn't miss it for the world," Bryce said a touch too brightly.

"And you've brought a friend, I see."

"More than a friend," Bryce said, sounding utterly sincere. "This is Melanie." He drew her closer to his side, making a point of showing they were a couple.

"I didn't know you were seeing anyone." The old man leaned forward eagerly.

"It was a chance meeting in a coffee shop. She was kind enough to let me buy her breakfast."

She bit her lip at the partial lie.

"Come closer. Let me meet the girl."

Girl? She might have taken offense except a man his age probably saw anyone under fifty as a girl or boy.

As they neared the head of the table, the young man—that must be Rory—stood while his lady friend remained seated.

Bryce slowed. "Chanice? I wasn't expecting you here."

He knew the woman?

"I thought I mentioned I was having dinner with my fiancé's family when I popped by today."

"Rory is your fiancé?" Bryce turned a glare on the man.

"Yes he is." The red lips pulled into a smug smile. "We met while I was out on the West Coast. Imagine our surprise when we found out he was related to the Elanrouxs, especially given how close our families are."

"Imagine that." Said flatly by Bryce.

"Small world, eh, boy? A fine choice my nephew has made, but it looks like you've also done well for yourself. Come a little closer, young lady. This old body isn't as spry as it used to be."

Melanie inched closer, a little daunted by the fierce blue gaze. She couldn't avoid slipping her hand into the callused one of the old man. He gripped her tightly and drew her closer, the strength at odds with the bundled body.

And did he...smell her?

He smells funny, too. Kind of like Bryce did, but it was hard to tell with the cloying perfume of the candles and other scents in the room.

"It's n-n-ice to meet you, s-sir," she managed to stammer.

"Please, call me Theo. After all, if you're dating my grandson you're almost family." The lips spread wide in the creased face. "And might I say, what a delight. It's been a while since I've met one of your kind."

Kind? Was this a jab at the fact she came from the wrong side of the tracks? She cast a startled glance at Bryce but he didn't seem to think anything was awry as he pulled out a chair for her at his grandfather's right hand.

The woman, Chanice, had the left.

For a moment, after everyone sat, silence hung thickly in the air and everyone stared at each other.

Kendrick was the one to break it. "Is my lord ready for his dinner?"

Theo clasped his hands. "Indeed. I find I have quite the appetite."

Dinner proved lavish, starting with a soup, a tomato bisque, with crunchy bread to dip.

Initially there was little conversation, the silence awkward. Melanie couldn't stand it. So she said something to the cousin that kept eyeing her. "How did you find out you were related to the Elanrouxs?" Probably a socially gauche move, yet this entire experience thus far seemed more fit for a soap opera than real life.

The blond man took a sip of wine before answering. "My father finally told me after my mother's death. He'd promised to keep it a secret so I wouldn't stop caring for her when I realized she wasn't my birth mother."

"I'm sorry to hear about your mother."

"It was hard," Rory said, "but finding new family,"—a blazing smile at Theo, a more rapier slick one for Bryce—"has helped me deal with the loss."

"I'm sure the money helped," Bryce muttered under his breath.

"No sad talk." Chanice jumped into the fray with a clap of her hands. "This is supposed to be happy dinner. I am sure I'm not the only one curious about how you and Bryce met. He mentioned a coffee shop. Do you work there?"

The rudeness might have startled Melanie if she'd not expected it. "At the moment, I'm between jobs, as I care for my mother."

"I don't believe I've met her," stated the old man.

"Count yourself lucky," she muttered, wondering why he'd even say that. Being the town's richest member didn't mean everyone living in it was a vassal that had to kiss his feet.

"So, I was thinking of touring the factory tomorrow," Rory tossed out.

Bryce immediately stiffened. "Why?"

"Just taking an interest in the family biz, cousin. After all, you and I are the only living heirs." Emphasis on the living.

"For now. We'll see what the blood work says."

The barely veiled threats had Melanie watching the men, her gaze bobbing between them.

"Have you made the plans for the wedding yet?" Theo asked, ignoring the tension.

"While I know my darling fiancée wanted something large and lavish, she's agreed to something smaller and intimate. We're planning something simple for next week that you and her family can attend, and then when we fly back west, we'll throw something a little more lavish."

"Next week?" Bryce barked.

"Is there a problem, cousin? I would think you'd be happy for me. After all, we both know all grandfather wants is for his bloodline to continue."

Bryce's jaw stiffened. "His true bloodline."

"What are you saying?" Rory glared.

"You know exactly what I'm saying. You're an imposter."

"And you're a spoiled boy who is whining because he can't win. Get over it. Maybe if you're nice to me, I'll let you work in the factory."

The tennis match of barbs turned tense.

Scree. Bryce shoved his chair back and stood, tension bristling through his body. "You'll never get your grubby paws on it."

"That's not up to you, is it?" Rory stood and faced Bryce.

"I won't let you steal my inheritance."

"How are you going to stop me? Gonna wave your great big rack and moo like a cow?"

The taunt made no sense, and yet, with a cry of rage, Bryce dove over the table and tackled Rory, their bodies crashing to the floor.

The sound of meaty thumps filled the air as fists flailed and found flesh.

Appalled, Melanie turned on Theo. "Aren't you going to do something?"

"Boys will be boys."

"This is sick." She yanked the napkin from her lap and tossed it onto the table before standing. "Family shouldn't be like this."

She stalked out of the room, not sure how she'd get home but desperate to leave.

The butler popped out of a room. "Can I help you, miss?"

"I need..." A cab? No money. "Nothing." It would take a while, but she'd walk.

She strutted out into the cool evening air, the briskness of it pimpling the skin on her arms. She'd made it past the ornate gates when the headlights illuminated her.

A car slowed to a stop beside her, and the door opened. Bryce leaned across, his hair tousled, his lip bloody, and growled, "Get in."

"No, thank you." She kept walking.

The car kept pace. "Don't be stubborn. You can't walk all the way home."

She didn't plan to. Once she got out of sight, she planned to change and run on four legs. "This isn't going to work."

"What are you talking about? Grandfather loved you."

Stopping, she stared at him, incredulous. "You've got to be kidding me."

"Stop moping and get in."

"I am not moping," said the woman who moped rather than get driven home.

Don't be stupid. Get in the car. After this farce, the least he could do was give her a ride home. She sat in the car and crossed her arms, determined to ignore him.

"You're cute when you're angry."

"Just drive," she snapped. But she couldn't help a warm glow at his words.

Jerk.

Stay strong. Don't give in to the charm.

And don't breathe, because every inhalation drugged her with his scent, muddled her thoughts.

What is happening to me?

Chapter 11

Bryce could feel her simmering beside him. He couldn't truly blame her. He'd lost control, let that dickwad bait him into acting. "Well, that went better than expected," Bryce declared when she hadn't said a word for a few miles.

She turned an incredulous gaze on him. "How do you figure that? You and Rory got in a fight."

"Yeah, but that was bound to happen at one point. The more important thing is grandfather liked you."

"Do you think?" She sounded uncertain. "I felt like such an imposter the whole time."

"Why?" he asked as he pulled to a stop in front of her place.

"That's a dumb question, or is your silver spoon so big you can't see it?"

He laughed. "I think you just accused me of being a snob." Which entertained him. Most women fawned over him endlessly, but Melanie had a down-to-earth attitude that wasn't meant to stroke his ego, which made the fact that every time he touched her and got near, and her pulse began racing quicker, it was because she truly was affected by him. Not his wealth. Not his stature.

It made a man swell—and not just with pride.

"It's not your fault," she teased, a hint of a smirk on her lips. "You were born that way." She hopped out of the car, not waiting for him to come around.

He could have driven away. After all she'd played her part for the night, yet he found himself reluctant for it to end. He caught up to her just outside the door to the building.

She whirled, her eyes bright, her lips parted. "What are you doing?"

"A gentleman, even a snob, always sees his date to the door."

"Even fake dates?"

"Most especially a fake one. After all, someone could be watching."

"Do you seriously think someone is spying on you?"

He wouldn't put it past his grandfather. "Most definitely"—he leaned closer to her—"which means we really should make this look real." Before she could protest, he pressed his mouth to hers.

A jolt of electricity went through him, not the real kind that came from sticking his tongue in a socket for fun, but the kind that slammed him with awareness. That woke his body to the fact that he desired this woman like he'd never desired anyone before.

She didn't shove him away, and so he deepened the embrace, coaxing her lips apart with his own, nibbling on the soft flesh, feeling the hot pants of her breath mingling with his own. His hands spanned her slim waist, and he drew her near. Near enough for her to feel the evidence of his arousal.

She kissed him back, shyly at first, but when he groaned, she grew bolder, letting her tongue slide along his, nibbling his mouth, craning on tiptoe just to reach him.

He curled his arm around her and lifted her off her feet, deepening the embrace, truly tasting her.

Needing her.

Who cared if they were predators on opposite sides? (And yes, moose were predators, deadly forest kings who ruled with sharp tines!)

Who cared if this relationship wasn't supposed to be real? It felt real and good and right and…

The shrill ring of his phone shattered the spell.

She shoved away from him and said, her voice high and breathy, "Good night, Bryce." Then she left him. Left him aching and hard.

Which meant he was annoyed when he answered his phone and barked, "This better be important."

"The factory is on fire."

Chapter 12

Sleep proved almost impossible. The couch purposely kept her awake. The lumps extra uncomfortable, the buttons on the cushions digging. Every single noise had her twitching, and Melanie couldn't even blame it on her mother. Martha had given her mother a sleeping pill, which would last the night, and gone home when Melanie insisted.

It was just Melanie and her thoughts.

Her tumultuous thoughts.

Only one person to blame for her restlessness: Bryce.

He kissed me.

What a kiss!

Reading about passion exploding and knees buckling and insides melting like gooey chocolate was one thing. To actually experience it? Damn. Had his phone not rung, who knew how far things might have gotten?

Not very far, seeing as how I don't even have a place to go with him. Somehow sneaking him in for a tryst on the couch with her mother in the other room just didn't sound romantic.

Probably for the best. *He and I shouldn't get involved.* She shouldn't forget this was a sham—no matter how hot the kiss. He was only using her to fool his grandfather while she used him to try and better her life.

It was the perfect arrangement, which meant she shouldn't muck it up with kisses and misplaced feelings. Keep it professional. Distant.

Of course, that was hard to remember when he showed up the next morning at her door, right behind the new nurse, as she bustled in.

Poor Bryce looked exhausted and dirty, his previously clean clothes covered in soot, smelling strongly of smoke.

"What happened?" she asked, slipping out of the apartment to speak with him in the hall. She didn't want him to see just how poorly she lived.

"Fire at the maple syrup plant."

"Oh no. Was anyone hurt?"

"No, and thankfully there wasn't much damage from the fire itself, but the smoke ruined all the pending batches of syrup, not to mention fucked up our production times. It will be weeks before we're cleared by the health inspectors to start producing again."

"What happened?"

He shrugged. "We don't know yet. Best guess is a careless smoker. But we won't know for sure until we get the fire marshal's report."

"I'm sorry. That's awful news." Which made her wonder why he showed up here instead of going home. "I'll understand if you want to call off our arrangement so you can handle this."

"What?" He appeared startled. "Not at all. I came here to ask if you're available for lunch today."

"Given the news of the factory, is your grandfather well enough for that?"

"Probably not, so good thing he won't be there. I was talking about a lunch with just the two of us."

The words filtered slowly. She blinked at him. "Us, as in alone?"

"Yes, alone. You do realize we also have to see each other outside of my grandfather's presence to make this work?"

"Of course." There he went with his paranoid conviction that people were watching. "I can do lunch. What should I wear?" Because the dilemma remained, she owned nothing.

"Something comfortable. I was thinking we'd have a picnic."

Only as she closed the door after planning a time, did she think of it. A picnic would have no audience. How exactly would this advance his cause with his grandfather? Shouldn't there be a witness or spying eyes to their fake budding romance?

Or perhaps he planned to immortalize it by taking images for social media. An intimate picnic would look great in that case.

Whatever the reason, she couldn't stem her excitement, and her mother noticed when she went in to say good morning after the nurse finished bathing and feeding her.

"You look awfully pleased with yourself." Maizie's gaze narrowed.

"It's a beautiful day."

"If you're not stuck in bed, dying, with a daughter so lazy she uses your money to hire help."

"It's not your money paying for it."

"Then whose?"

Despite knowing the probable reaction, she said it anyhow. "My boyfriend."

"Whore!" The word emerged quick and harsh.

"Am not."

"Then why would he agree to pay for it? You must have given him sexual favors."

"We've only kissed."

"But he'll be expecting more. Selling your body so that you can avoid being a proper daughter," Maizie sneered. "You're a slut, just like your father."

"I'd rather be like him. At least he was smart enough to leave," Melanie snapped.

"Is that what you think? That he left?" Maizie's

lips twisted, and her eyes sparked with malice. "I was the one who took off on him."

"What?" Melanie froze as her mother's words filtered.

"You heard me. I left him. The bloody bastard thought he could just toss me aside for that other woman. As if I meant nothing. I showed him."

It turned her blood cold to hear, but she had to know. "Did you ever tell him where we went? Where I was?"

"Never! I took off with you and never looked back. The bastard never got to hold his precious little girl." Smugness dripped from the words.

My dad never left me.

The horrifying truth slapped Melanie, and she couldn't stand to look at Maizie's face any longer. Her whole world had just been dumped on its ass.

The knock on the door saved her, and she fled the room with its ugly revelation, flinging open the door and brushing past Bryce with a terse, "Let's go."

She didn't say much during the drive, and after his attempted, "What's wrong?" and her snapped, "None of your business. It's personal," he stopped trying. He just drove them in silence and parked by the woods.

Woods that she knew. The same forest where she'd recently gone for a run and encountered that giant moose and then those scary wolves.

In her mind, hackles rose, and she dug her nails into her palm lest the yowl building within release.

"Are you sure it's safe to be here?" She couldn't exactly tell him what had happened so she had to settle for, "I hear there's been wolves sighted."

Being a man, he didn't appear bothered at all about big hairy creatures that could tear his arm off. "Don't worry about them. They won't bother you while you're with me. Come on."

Still, she bit her lower lip and worried. What was he implying? Was he armed? Had someone culled the pack and eliminated the threat? If yes, then it made any future treks to this forest to stretch her furry paws a bad idea. If there were hunters and poachers around, they'd probably love to bag a lynx.

Perhaps they were watching right now, eyes pressed to a scope, sighting their next victim.

Slap. Her cat gave her a mental whack. *You're not going into the woods as a cat.* She was here to have a picnic like a normal person. A hunter wouldn't shoot a woman.

From the trunk, Bryce pulled out a hamper, a real wicker one with a handle, and a folded blanket. She tucked her hands in her jean pockets as she watched, her inner kitty twitching, not out of fear but eagerness.

It would be nice to go for a run in daylight.

She'd never tried that before, too scared someone would see her. Besides, how would she explain that to Bryce? *I'm different than you.*

He wouldn't believe her. Then she'd show him. Then he'd run off screaming and get a gun.

And then where would she be? Possibly stuffed and mounted as a trophy.

Best to keep her secret and shove her longing deep down inside. She placated her inner feline with, *If there are no hunters, then maybe later we'll come back and see if we can catch a fish.*

Although this time, if they did succeed in snaring one, she might close her human mind to the slurpy gooey eating part of it.

Bryce slammed the trunk of his car shut and tucked the blanket under an arm. He used that same arm to carry the hamper, leaving a free hand to grab hers.

She almost yanked it away, mostly because the jolt of awareness immediately brought a flush to her body.

"What did we say about flinching?" he teased, lacing her fingers with his, allowing no escape.

"That wasn't flinching. It was preserving my bubble."

"Relax and let me in. I won't bite."

He might not, but she could. And scratch too. Meow.

"You come here often?" she asked, striving for nonchalance in spite of a racing heart.

"As much as I can. I find the forest to be peaceful. The one place I can be myself."

She understood that all too well. At times, when she shifted at night, the freedom to be herself, her true self, was bittersweet.

"Is it a protected parkland?"

"Protected, yes, but not by the government. My family owns this."

"All of it?" she asked, because she'd gotten the impression it extended for miles and miles.

"Three thousand nine hundred and sixty-three acres, to be exact."

"Wow. But then again, I guess that makes sense." She pointed to the trees. "Sap for the syrup."

"Not from this section, but you are correct. We have a dedicated section for collection. Our foresters keep it thriving, ensuring any sickly trees are immediately cared for."

"You use pesticides?"

He visibly shuddered. "Perish the thought. We use more natural methods, culling as the last resort."

"You sound like you're really into the whole maple syrup thing."

"I am." He smiled down at her. "It's not only lucrative, it's delicious."

The way he said it caused her to shiver. To have that applied to—

She ignored the direction of her thoughts. "How far are we going?" Because if she wasn't mistaken, they neared the stream.

"Not far. You should recognize it. It is, after all, where we first unofficially met."

The word brought a chill. *What is he saying?*

She'd never seen Bryce in the woods. The only time she'd been here she'd been shifted.

Think of it.

Her mind shied. "It's peaceful here."

"Indeed it is. I thought you might need it."

"Why?"

"I was talking to Martha. She happened to mention your mother is a tad difficult."

A noise left her. "Yeah, you could say that."

"I know about difficult family members." He squeezed her hand, a moment of shared understanding that eased something inside her.

When they emerged from the forest, the sound of the stream filled her senses, as did the smell of it. She closed her eyes and breathed deep, filling her lungs, letting herself relax.

This was nice. For a fake date.

"Here we are." He tossed the blanket to the ground and spread it. He set the basket in the middle and, with a wave of his hand, invited her to sit.

They then proceeded to have a normal picnic. The food in the hamper was beyond delicious: thick-cut sandwiches layered with smoky ham, Dijon mustard, and Swiss cheese, plus crispy lettuce. The kettle chips were salty and crunched. A thermos of lemon iced tea went down smooth. He'd even thought to bring some freshly baked cookies for dessert.

It might have been the best meal she'd ever had. The company might have had a lot to do with that. Despite his innate arrogance, Bryce had a quick wit and charm that kept her on her toes as they conversed.

He flirted outrageously, probably something he did with every woman he met, and yet, she still enjoyed it.

His intelligence shone through as he spoke, as did his love for this land, the company, and even his ornery grandfather.

It was all too easy to forget that this was a sham. If only it weren't.

The fall afternoon unfolded perfectly, the temperature just right, the sun a dancing delight on her skin. She turned her face into it and not for the first time wished she could run free in its rays.

"Want to go for a nature walk?" Bryce asked.

She opened her eyes as a shadow fell over her. Bryce stood and, as she watched, began to unbutton his shirt.

"What are you doing?" Because she could have sworn he'd asked her to walk, and most people stayed clothed for that.

"Preserving my clothes. Aren't you going to strip, too?"

"Uh, no. I prefer to keep my clothes on when going for a stroll."

He canted his head. "You weren't wearing any clothes the other night."

The comment confused. "What are you talking about?"

"The first time we unofficially met." At her blank face, he sighed. "By the river. You can stop pretending you don't remember meeting my majestic moose."

The conversation turned from odd to disturbing. "You have a pet moose?"

"Not a pet. Me. I'm the moose."

The words finally sank in, as did their meaning. Still, it couldn't be. *I thought I was the only one.*

A concept that made her inner kitty chuff.

Ask him. "You can change into an animal?"

"Of course I can. Hold on a second, are you telling me you didn't know?" Now it was his turn to look puzzled.

She took a deep breath. "I've never met someone else that could. I thought I was alone."

The whites of his eyes showed in his surprise. "Alone? Why would you think that? Didn't your parents teach you any of your heritage..." The words trailed off. "Holy shit, your mom never knew and—"

"My dad left." Her head ducked as her shoulders lifted and fell. "I found out by accident when I was a teenager."

"Damn. That must have been confusing."

More like terrifying for a young girl who'd run off after yet another fight with her mother, feeling something wild beating in her chest, something fighting to get free.

"I learned how to deal with it. But I never knew there was others like me."

"Didn't you smell them? We're very distinct."

"I've smelled something, with some people." Her gaze met his briefly, but she couldn't handle the directness of it, so she quickly dropped it. "But it's not exactly like you can go up to them and say, 'Hey, you smell like an animal.'" She peeked at him.

His lips quirked. "It is considered rather gauche."

"So, there's more people like me out there?"

"More than you can imagine."

"And you're a moose?" The very idea boggled the mind. Wolves, she could fathom. Bears, too. Even big cats like lions and tigers and a lynx like her, but a moose? She snickered.

"What's so funny?"

"You're a moose."

"And? You're a cat."

"But really, a moose?" She burst out laughing and kept laughing the more disgruntled he looked.

"I don't understand your entertainment. We are fine and noble creatures."

She chortled. "Let me guess, it's all about the size of the rack."

"According to my several times removed cousin Boris, yes, but he's the oddball in the family."

"You mean there's more of you? So, do you get together like a flock of meese? Do you like whip out your antlers and compare sizes?"

"Don't mess with the rack," he growled.

"Or what? You'll waggle them at me?" She couldn't help but tease, and he didn't appreciate it.

He dove at her.

Chapter 13

The laughter was bad enough. The mockery too, but then she did the unthinkable. She held up her fingers to her crown and waggled them.

Mocking him.

Bryce charged Melanie, lifted her off her feet, and held her high, glaring at her. She didn't look scared at all. She squealed and continued to laugh, deeply and joyfully.

After her somberness of before, he couldn't stand to be the reason why it stopped—even if he was the butt of her joke.

But he did know of one way to silence her that would make him happy.

He kissed her, and it turned out it wasn't a fluke or his imagination. The touch of their lips truly was an explosion for his senses. Every nerve ending in his body awakened.

Ignited.

Desire flowed like a molten river through his veins.

He deepened the kiss, parting her lips with his tongue, tasting the bitter sweetness of the iced tea, feeling her soften in his arms and return his embrace.

As he held her aloft, she wrapped her arms around his neck, hugging him close, their bodies pressing tight. Clothes impeded skin-to-skin contact. He growled as he rubbed his hands over the fabric of her shirt, tucked into her jeans.

She wiggled until he set her down. For a moment, he thought she might have changed her mind. Yet, she held his gaze as she tugged her shirt free, peeling it off, leaving her clad in her bra and jeans. Her hands went to the button on her pants next. Pop. The loop opened, the zipper slid down, his mouth went dry.

A coy smile pulled her lips as she shrugged them off, her cotton panties—a pale pink and full hipped—the sexiest thing he'd ever seen.

"Come here." He crooked a finger, eager to touch her, feel her.

A shake of her head and a giggle meant a contagious mirth. She teased and, before his eyes changed, but before she did, she chortled, "You'll have to catch me first."

While he'd changed many a time, and in the presence of others, he found himself fascinated anew by the process. Skin replaced by fur. A body that reshaped as if momentarily elastic. The whole physical makeup flipped into something new, leaving only familiar eyes.

A wink.

Then off she dashed, her powerful hind legs propelling her away from him.

Shit.

He quickly stripped and morphed into his shape, bellowing a cry of exultation as he felt his powerful rack spring from hiding, the mechanics of it a magic no amount of science and medicine could explain.

It just was.

Off he bounded, his four-legged, long stride taking him along the same trail as her. He had no need to stop and smell. Her scent was imprinted on him, almost visible to follow.

She led him on a merry chase. Weaving through tall trees. Dashing through a meadow, the tip of her furry butt winking out of sight as she fled into the woods.

Splash. Furry paws hit water as she thought to lose him in a thin stream, but his height meant he saw the faint imprint of a paw in mud where she exited the water.

He leapt over the creek and hit the other side, charging through the woods, knowing this land better than her. He herded her, weaving left and right, forcing her into a direction.

Ahead was a stony outcrop. Too steep even for a nimble cat to climb.

Only when he had her cornered did he change shapes, stalking toward her, body tense with anticipation. She changed as well, fur smoothing into skin, nice skin. Shapely flesh, the kind he wanted to touch and kiss all over.

He could see the rapid beat of her pulse, the flushed heat in her cheeks. He grabbed her in his arms, the hot contact of their flesh a sensual override on his system.

The temptation of her lips meant he dipped his head to kiss her, deeply and passionately. His hands roamed her frame, learning her curves, marking them with his touch, wanting to imprint himself on her. To have her bear his scent.

He took her mouth. Claimed it. Ran his tongue along the seam as his hands roamed the skin of her back.

Lusciously lean, yet curved in the right places. Her waist an indent that flared over hips. Her ass a taut pleasure to grab. The hardness of his erection pressed against her lower belly. Straining and ready.

He wanted her desperately, and the scent of her arousal, the sweetest of perfumes, showed she wanted him too…so why did she pull away?

Why did she chew that lower lip instead of nibbling on him?

Why did it sound like she just said they needed to slow down because…

He might have given his head a little shake. "What did you just say?"

"I said I'm a virgin."

Chapter 14

How to stay a virgin. Tell a guy kissing you like you're the sexiest thing alive you've never been intimate with a man before. Admit to a guy, naked and hard for you, that you've still got a cherry.

A cherry that probably wouldn't be popped by the guy backing away, panic brimming in his eyes.

"You're joking, right?" he said with a note of consternation.

She shrugged. "Nope."

"But how? That's impossible. I mean look at you." He gestured to her body.

A compliment, and yet, his admiration of her body didn't bring back the kisses.

"It's not because I wanted to stay a virgin." Especially in her teens when her hormones raged. "But I was worried that someone would find out about my secret." Especially since she wasn't sure if she could control herself in the heat of the moment. What if she changed? It was one thing to leave nail marks in a man's back, but claw marks? That might be a little harder to explain.

"But...but..." He seemed completely thrown by the news.

"I guess it makes a difference to you."

"Yes. No. I mean, I don't fucking know. It was one thing if we got together and had some fun, but you're a virgin." Baldly stated.

"You don't have to say it like that. It's not a disease." He couldn't catch it. Yet, the reassurance didn't bring him back. He kept his distance.

"We should get going." He turned around and presented a very fine ass. An ass walking away.

Rather unexpected. So much for being honest. However, she kind of felt obligated given he'd notice at one point when he breached her hymen and there was blood everywhere.

A few paces away, he turned around and sighed loudly. "We should probably change back, or it will be a painful walk."

That was all that was said during their trot back to their picnic blanket. Then again, what could they say as their animals?

"Moo."

"Meow. Hiss."

Yeah, not exactly conducive for working things out. As he trotted back, she eyed his broad back and wondered what he'd do if she jumped on top and held on for a ride. At least then she'd get some kind of action.

Back at their picnic stop, they dressed in silence.

Tears brimmed in her eyes. Rejection stung.

So, it was with a bit of shock that she yelped when he grabbed her and pulled her close to mutter, "I can see what you're thinking."

"Really?"

"You think I don't want you."

"Can you blame me? I just got dropped like a hot potato."

"I'll admit, you took me by surprise. But what's happening between us isn't over. Not by a long shot."

Funny how that sounded like a threat—and yet heat curled in her belly.

Chapter 15

Melanie didn't say much as he drove her home. He was tongue-tied, too.

A virgin. They were kind of like unicorns. Known of but never seen. At least by him.

He didn't know what to do with a virgin.

Especially one that wouldn't look him in the eye and jumped out of his car and ran to her apartment building. He almost chased after, but his phone dinged.

Kendrick messaged him. *Your grandfather wishes to speak with you.*

Seeing her tail end vanish inside, things unresolved between them, Bryce was tempted to blow him off.

Melanie needed him. And he didn't mean for sex.

She didn't know what being a shifter was. How the hell did that happen? Their kind was careful about the babies they made, especially with humans. Someone had to teach her.

I should teach her. Teach her about her heritage. Teach her how to stay safe. Teach her the ways of the flesh.

Because she was untouched.

Pure.

Mine.

Shit. As he stared blankly, he had a revelation. He wanted to make their relationship into a real one. Forget faking it. Forget grandfather even.

She is the one. His mate. His woman. He was sure of it.

And he'd blown her off because she'd never had sex.

Bang. Bang. Bang. His forehead hit the steering wheel repeatedly as his stupidity slapped him.

She'd been ready to offer herself to him. Chosen him! And he'd rejected her.

Ugh.

I have to fix this.

Buzz. His phone stirred angrily. He stared at the building. Perhaps it was best he gave her a little bit of time. While he tried to figure out a way to apologize, he might as well go see what the old man wanted.

The entire way home, he tried to think of ways to apologize.

Jewelry? He could see her throwing it at him.

Chocolate? Was it cats or dogs who were allergic?

I could just be a man about this and kiss her until she forgives me. A scenario that he wholeheartedly approved of. He almost turned around to try it, but he'd already arrived home. Best take care of his grandfather first.

Entering the bedroom, he found his grandfather in bed, sitting upright, blanket tucked around him, his face an unhealthy shade of red.

"About time you showed up, boy."

"I was busy."

"Get unbusy. We have a situation," grandfather bellowed.

"One that's worth you having a heart attack over?" Bryce asked, not liking his grandfather's agitation.

"Someone is trying to take over the company," the old man blurted out.

"What?" Bryce frowned. "Take over how?"

"Buying up all our stock, that's how."

"Who is?"

"Those bloody knock-off piss vendors, that's who." For the uninformed, that was anyone not selling pure maple syrup made from a tree. Savages.

"But you own most of the shares." Grandfather had forty-five percent. Bryce had gotten ten percent on his twenty-first birthday.

"Most isn't a majority."

"Yeah, but I've got enough to keep it from happening."

"Unless they get to you." Grandfather glared at him.

The paranoia was strong today. "You're out of your fucking mind if you think I'd sell them."

"You might not sell them, but you could vote against me. Vote with them." Spat with disgust.

Bryce sighed. "No. I wouldn't. Where the hell would you get a stupid idea like that?"

"No one." Said rather quickly.

Bryce's gaze narrowed. "No one? Or a certain moocher?"

"He's not asked me for anything."

"But he's been in your ear nattering, apparently. Why the fuck would you listen to him? He's not even related to us."

"We don't know that. I'm still waiting for the lab report."

"Which is taking a hell of a long time."

"They had issues."

"How convenient," was Bryce's sarcastic drawl.

"Worry less about Rory and more about yourself. How are things with that girl? Kendrick says you went on a picnic. That's not how you impress a lady."

"Melanie loved the picnic." It was the cold shoulder afterwards she took exception too. If only he could rewind time and not freeze like a moose in headlights.

"Sources say she stormed off when you dropped her off."

"Spying on me?" He kind of expected it, but to have it baldly stated...

"More like kindly kept informed by passersby."

Bryce raked a hand through his hair as he paced. "Unbelievable. We had a bit of a tiff. My fault and I intend to fix it."

"Better hope you can. Tick tock, boy."

He whirled and glared at his grandfather. "Don't start again. You can't just expect me to wed and bed her in two minutes flat."

"Not my fault you chose a stranger. Here's to hoping you can seal the deal in time."

"How about giving a damn about whether or not she's the right woman for me?"

"Any woman with birthing hips will do."

"You're fucking unbelievable." Bryce stormed out, annoyed at the pressure, annoyed at himself for screwing up, and even more annoyed that someone had caught him looking annoyed.

Moooo-oooo. He could have bellowed.

"Looking a touch agitated, there, cousin." Out in the hall, Rory smirked, and Bryce clenched his fist by his side lest he wipe it clean from his face.

"And you're looking smug," Bryce spat. "Is that because you think you've fooled everyone into thinking your story is true?"

"The old man believes it. You heard him. I am the spitting image of his sister."

"Doesn't mean shit. I think you planned this, you and Chanice." It made sense. She couldn't get Bryce, but still wanted to get her hands on the fortune. This was her version of payback.

"I'm hurt." Rory clapped a hand over his chest. "It's one thing to accuse me, but to accuse my darling fiancée? I'm crushed."

"Did your fiancée happen to mention we used to date?" At the tightening of the muscle in Rory's jaw, Bryce knew this was news to him. "I also dumped her. She's been trying ever since to get back in this house and in my bed. Guess she had to settle for a pale imitation instead."

"Why you fucking—" Rory bristled and invaded his space. Toe to toe, glaring.

"What? Come on. Bring it." He crooked his fingers and beckoned.

A throat cleared. "Excuse me, sirs, but given the fragile state of Master Theodore, could you take your altercation elsewhere?" Kendrick interrupted with a cool and calm voice, but Bryce knew from experience not to irritate the man.

Rory didn't. "Get your ass back into the kitchen and stay out of this," Rory snarled, and made the mistake of watching Bryce.

Kendrick clocked him and then stared at the unconscious heap on the floor. "Appalling manners. What should I do with him?"

Put him out with the trash? Grandfather probably wouldn't like it. "Put him to bed. We should get the results of the DNA anytime now. Which means he'll soon be gone."

And so was Bryce a few minutes later after a phone call from Maizie's nurse.

Chapter 16

She's dead.

Disbelief and numbness kept Melanie staring at the bed long after they'd taken her mother's body away. Despite knowing it would happen, her mother being gravely sick, it still shocked her to walk in the door and find the nurse working on her non-responsive mother.

But the nurse couldn't revive her, and neither could the paramedics who arrived minutes later. The disease had finally killed Maizie, silenced that shrill voice forever, and Melanie didn't feel the relief she expected.

Didn't feel much of anything at all.

No, wait. Untrue. There was a twinge of guilt that, while she'd been out cavorting with Bryce, her mother had died, alone.

Being here wouldn't have changed a thing. Except

she could have sung a song. "Na Na Hey Hey Kiss Him Goodbye" came to mind.

The wicked witch was dead leaving her...free.

For the first time in her life, Melanie was alone, and beholden to no one.

Scary.

Stomach-clenching.

Ripe with possibility.

Exhilarating.

I can do whatever I like. Go wherever I want.

Melanie could even try and find the father that was stolen from her by a selfish mother.

Now, if only I knew his name.

"Melanie? Where are you?"

It didn't surprise her Bryce had come. After all, the nurse probably called him the moment she left.

He found her sitting in the chair by her mother's empty bed.

"Melanie, I'm so sorry."

"Why?" she asked, cocking her head. "You never met her, which was probably a lucky thing for you. She wasn't a nice woman. She was mean, as a matter of fact. The world is better off without her."

"You don't mean that."

"Actually, I do. You have no idea just how horrible she was to me growing up. And even as an adult. Not one kind word ever left her lips. Ever. Now she's gone. No more, 'Melanie, you lazy cow, fetch me this.' No more calling me a whore because I looked in a man's direction."

"I'm sure she loved you—"

She shook her head as she finally vocalized the thing she'd thought for so long. "No. No, she didn't. A mother who loves her child doesn't constantly hurt her. Maizie was never a mother to me. And now that she's gone, I'm free. Free to do whatever I like and go wherever I please."

"What do you mean, free? I thought we had a deal."

Her lips twisted. "Ah, yes, the proposition from my billionaire moose. I guess you didn't hear the news."

"What news?"

"The nurse told me. It's all over social media. The fact that Rory lied. He's not your cousin. At least not by your Aunt Trixie. Because his mother is still alive."

His eyes widened. "What? How do you know this? We're still waiting on the DNA tests."

"The media did what you couldn't. They dug past his backstory to get the real truth. Apparently, he's Malcolm Rory Beauchamp Lupin."

"Lupin, as in the fucking Lupin family who owns Lip Smackn' Syrup and Candy, Incorporated?"

"One and the same. Beauchamp is his mother's maiden name. A mother very much alive. As is his father." A soap opera come to life. Melanie had only partially listened as the nurse babbled on about the scandal.

Propositioned by the Billionaire Moose

"Son of a bitch." Bryce whirled and paced. "Why, though? Why pretend? He had to know it wouldn't fly."

"Don't ask me." She shrugged. "But anyhow, with him discredited, that means we don't need to continue with this charade." It meant the brief fantasy was over. It hurt more than expected.

"What if it weren't a charade? What if we made it real?"

For a moment, she allowed herself to imagine it, falling for this man, marrying him. Her, a nobody with no family, no money. Impossible. "We both know you don't want to get tied down. Now you don't have to. You can go back to being a happy bachelor, and I'll leave."

"To go where?"

"Anywhere but here." She wrinkled her nose at the room she'd grown to hate.

"I won't let you leave." He grabbed her. "We made a deal."

Why did he insist? "Let me go." She struggled in his grip, holding on to the hot tears, tears over a man she couldn't have.

"I don't want to let you go," he growled. "Not now, not ever."

"You heard the girl!" a voice boomed. "Unhand her!"

The interruption meant they both gaped at the big man standing in the doorway, his eyes blazing.

"Who the fuck are you?" snapped Bryce, releasing her to face the stranger.

"Kieran, her father."

And he might have said more, but that was when she decided to kiss the floor.

Chapter 17

For a moment, Bryce and this stranger stared at Melanie, and then they jostled to see who would pick her up off the floor.

Hand slapping ensued along with some growling. "Get your filthy hooves off my daughter."

His daughter? Could it be?

Much as Bryce wanted to call the man a liar, there was no mistaking the smell. Feline. Familiar feline, as in another lynx. What were the chances?

Bryce leaned back on his haunches as the man scooped Melanie into his arms and stared down at her, his features soft with love, but also marked by pain.

"Why are you here?" Bryce asked. Why now, after all this time?

"I'm here by accident. I was coming after my nephew. He's doing something stupid, again. The boy is rash. Doesn't always think. I'm here to bring him back. Except I got distracted by a scent. *Her* scent." His gaze turned soft as he stared at Melanie. "The spitting image of her mother—"

"I don't think that's a compliment," Bryce interjected. "You might not know this, but her mother wasn't exactly kind toward her."

"Maizie." The other man growled the name. "A pity I can't kill her twice. Stealing my child."

"So, you knew about Melanie?"

"Is that her name?" Kieran appeared startled. "We'd planned to call her Tanya. Only Maizie kidnapped her before we'd even signed the certificate."

"Hold on." Bryce shook his head. "Are you saying—"

"That Maizie wasn't her mother." The man's lip curled. "No. She was a psychotic mistake. I was drunk; we had sex. Once." Spoken quite firmly. "I told her afterwards it didn't mean anything, but the woman stalked me. Harassed me even after I met and impregnated my true mate, Jasmin. Maizie couldn't handle it. She stole our precious daughter."

"Stole?" The word erupted from Melanie. "Do you mean to tell me Maizie—"

Kieran's gaze shot to his daughter. "That *woman* was no relation to you. She was a kidnapper. A sadist. She stole the most precious thing Jasmin and I had."

"My real mother is..." The soft words came from

Melanie, who lay in her father's arms, looking vulnerable, her expression soft with hopefulness.

A sadness flitted through the man's eyes. "No, sweetheart. Unfortunately, your mother passed. The shock of losing you was just too much. She left this world about a year after you were abducted."

A sound escaped her.

Kieran hugged her tight. "I'm sorry, darling. You have no idea how much it pains me to hurt you."

The tautness of her body showed her hesitation, and her voice emerged in a hushed whisper. "You're my father?"

Eyes, the same as Melanie's, glistened with moisture. "I'm your daddy, sweetheart, and I promise, from now on, you'll never have to go through life without me by your side."

But...Bryce wanted to be the one Melanie relied on, her face on the pillow beside him. He cleared his throat. Time to insert himself into the situation. "What an interesting turn of events."

Direct yellow eyes set beneath thick gray brows perused him. Judged. Bryce might have come up wanting.

Kieran snarled, "Who the heck are you? And why the hell are you still here?" The man only needed a T-shirt that read: "Have daughter, will kill."

The rule of thumb when meeting another alpha, stand up or bow down.

Bryce didn't ever give in. His shoulders squared. He held out a hand. "Bryce Elanroux."

The rapier gaze didn't waver, and there was no handshaking. "Kieran Graysmoke," replied Melanie's father. "And I'm going to tell you, as a courtesy, to keep your filthy hooves off my girl. Or else." The last part spoken in a lower octave.

Bryce sighed. "What is it with people using that threat? What are you going to do? Attack me? Seems rather extreme. And I will have you know I'm never dirty. Kendrick would be appalled if we left the house less than perfectly groomed." Butlers had to maintain a certain standing among their peers. Letting their employers look less than perfect and they'd somehow failed the brotherhood. "And anything Melanie and I do will be consensual and none of your business."

Melanie bit her lip, fighting a smile.

Kieran sputtered. "There will be no business with my daughter. I know all about your family and their womanizing ways. My brother-in-law told me everything."

"Excuse me?" A puzzled note entered the query. "Who is your brother-in-law, and what does he know?" Had Bryce missed an important fact?

"My brother-in-law, Jack Lupin, and you've met his son, Rory."

"The imposter," Bryce sneered. "Didn't you hear? His plan failed."

"Did you call him an imposter?" Kieran snorted. "Rory won't fail because that boy is more an heir than you are. He's Theo Elanroux's by-blow. That big-racked bastard seduced Lupin's mate and impregnated her."

The news slapped him. He recoiled. "Impossible. You lie."

A wry smile pulled the man's lips. "I was just as skeptical when I found out. But it's true. Rory Lupin is Theo's son." Making him Bryce's uncle. "Rory is your cousin by marriage, darling," he told Melanie.

Melanie appeared excited by the discovery; meanwhile, Bryce was still reeling. He had to refute this garbage. "For Rory to be my cousin means my grandfather would have cheated on my nana." Which was something he didn't even want to contemplate. "He loved her."

"He did, and he also loved other women. Rory's mother wasn't the first. He was a rake in his day. Rory is living evidence."

"So, why is this only coming out now?" Why wait almost thirty years?

"Jack didn't want people to know, a pride thing, especially since Rory is the only child he and his wife ever had."

"What changed?"

Kieran shrugged. "Rory found out."

"Found and pretended to be Trixie's kid? Why?"

"He wanted to meet his biological father and felt this would be a better way of gauging his worth."

A twisted logic. "Who raised him?" Curiosity made Bryce ask.

"His mother and my brother-in-law. They live on the West Coast. Jack pretended for years the boy was his. Until his doctor ran some routine tests and the blood work gave away the fact Rory couldn't be his. Things were never the same between Rory and his father after that."

"Did my grandfather know about him?" Had he compounded the crime of his infidelity by abandoning his son?

"Theo never knew. Would have kept on not knowing if Rory hadn't decided it was time to come meet the man."

"And go after my inheritance."

Kieran's gaze narrowed. "Is it really yours? Rory is his son, and Theo is dying. Who do you think the courts will choose to inherit?"

"The DNA test will show he's not related." A lie was easier to believe.

"The lab has finished their checking. It took longer because they redid the test several times. Go ahead, give them a call."

The room spun, and when Bryce's phone buzzed, a peek showed a text from the lab, and the first line in the preview box said three damning words: Paternity is confirmed.

He walked out, not the same moose who'd gone in.

Bryce left Melanie, who'd gone from nothing to everything.

I have nothing to offer her.

Nothing but myself.

He wasn't sure if that was enough.

Chapter 18

It didn't take a genius to see the news hit Bryce hard. Not only was Rory related to him, but he was the actual son of his grandfather. A twist no one expected.

So many revelations, all at once, important ones.

Unable to handle some of it, Bryce walked out without a word.

A step forward. A jerking halt. She stared after him, wanting to run after Bryce to console him, but how could she leave the father she'd just found? She cast a glance at the man she'd only just found. His expression a mirror golden gaze.

He had answers for her. Could she really run away to help Bryce? What could she give Bryce? They'd only come together as part of a deal to save his heritage. If it weren't for the proposition, they would have never spent any time together.

He doesn't need me. A thought that hurt.

She turned away from the empty doorway and faked a bright smile for her father. "Tell me everything. Tell me about my family."

Over coffee at a shop down the street, they talked, and talked.

She got to see pictures of her mother, stored on her father's phone. Bittersweet, especially given the uncanny resemblance. *That's my smile. My head tilt.* She also got to hear stories of the life she could have had growing up. The cabin in the mountains where her parents lived. The extended family she'd meet. More lynx like her, because she'd inherited the gene from her dad. But apparently she should expect to meet some wolves too, because her mother used to be a shifter as well.

"So, you're all shifters?" she asked.

"Most of us. There are a few cubs that never truly change, but carry the gene. We try to keep close tabs on all the family in case they're late bloomers or their kids inherit. Nothing worse than coming of age not knowing what you are."

"It was scary the first time," Melanie admitted.

"I'll bet it was." The big calloused hands covered her own. "But don't worry. You won't ever have to be alone again. Once we go home, I'll teach you everything you need to know."

"Go? With you?" She blinked. In all the commotion of meeting her father, she'd not really grasped what his arrival might mean.

"You didn't want to stay, did you?" He didn't need to remind her of the shabby apartment for her to understand what he meant.

Why would she stay in that place of hatred? She owed nothing to the woman who'd stolen her. She wanted to forget. But leaving meant ditching Bryce. She'd made a promise to him, a promise she'd shirked by letting him leave.

How utterly selfish of me. The man was hurting, and she'd let him run off.

"I want to come. I do, but I have to take care of some things here first."

"This is about that womanizer, isn't it?" Her father's expression darkened. "Stay away from that bull. You heard what his grandfather did."

But Bryce wasn't Theo. People should be judged on their merits, not their bloodline. "He needs my help."

"His idea of help probably involves seduction." She didn't reply, but her expression must have indicated something. "Like grandfather, like grandson. He's a user. A rake."

"I'll be the judge of that."

"Stubborn like your mother." Spoken gruffly yet fondly. "If you're going to stay here, then I guess we'd better find something more suitable than where you are right now." His lip curled.

"We?" she asked.

"Yes, we, sweetheart. You didn't really think after finding you I'd leave, did you?" He shook his head and smiled. "I meant what I said. I'm here to stay, and the moment that suave moose hurts you, let me know. I'll take care of him." Her father's fist slammed into his palm.

"Thank you...Daddy."

They might have both cried a bit after that. Good tears, the kind that meant something broken was healing.

It didn't take long to pack her belongings. They'd mostly stayed in her bag from college, no room in the closet or dresser for her. The entire time, her father watched, lips pressed tight, angry, and she could guess why.

How it must hurt to see how she'd lived.

When she was done collecting her things, she didn't pause to say a dramatic goodbye to the hellhole she'd stayed in for the past few months. Melanie was going to look forward from now on.

Not back.

And her new attitude about life meant she was ready to take some new steps. To boldly go where she'd never gone before. The resolve meant she had to track down a moose.

Alone. Because her daddy wouldn't want to see what she planned to do next.

Chapter 19

The bottle of maple whiskey did little to dull his emotions. It was over.

Bryce had been dealt blow after blow in one day. First finding out Rory was the closet male heir. There was no doubt in his mind what his grandfather would do. It was what any man would do, discovering he had a direct descendent.

There goes my career, my life's work. The fact that he was young enough to start over didn't manage to pummel its way past his moroseness. Maybe later it would, but for now, he would damned well wallow.

Because he'd lost.

And then to add insult to injury, Melanie had found her true family. A father that wanted to take her away.

She made a deal with me. A deal when she was desperate and vulnerable. She had no need of it now.

No need of me. Hell, the deal wasn't even on the table anymore. There was no legacy left for him even if he did marry and pop out a kid.

He had nothing. Nothing to offer Melanie.

Knock. Knock. He swiveled in his chair to glare at the door. No one should have been around, the place shut down until the cleaners got through with it. No one here but him and his personal demons. *Knock.* Through the frosted glass, he could see a shadow.

"Who is it?" he snapped. "Go away."

"No." Her soft voice hit him before the scent of her did. She stepped into his office, beautiful and frail, yet with an inner strength that awed. She'd gone through so much and remained strong. She'd gone from the lowest place in her life to the highest, and he was happy for her—even if it put her out of reach.

"I guess you came to tell me you're leaving," he said, taking another sip of the sweet whiskey liquor.

"Actually, I am here to tell you I'm not going anywhere until the deal is done. I made a promise, and I intend to keep it."

At her declaration, he snorted. "Kind of pointless now, going on. Rory's the true heir. A secret maple son returned to the fold."

"I'm sure your grandfather won't leave you out in the cold."

"Maybe not, but this"—he waved his hand around—"isn't truly mine. It belongs to my uncle. And his future children."

Her gaze narrowed. "Is that it, then? You're just going to give up?"

"Not giving up, conceding defeat. Maybe I won't be the next maple syrup baron, but I'm sure there's something out there for me. What about you? When do you leave with your father?" His heart shriveled as he waited for her reply.

"I already told you I'm not leaving. I have unfinished business."

He wanted to throw the glass as frustration welled inside. "The deal is off. Don't stay on my account. I certainly don't plan to."

"This isn't about the deal. This is about me and what I want."

The way she said it, the way she drew near, her gaze steady on him, almost hungry.

Hope fluttered in his breast. "What do you want?" The words emerged low and gruff.

"I want you to finish what you started in the woods."

"But you're a—"

"If you say the word virgin, I will hurt you. Don't you get it? I don't want to be a virgin anymore."

"So, you just want to get rid of it, and want to use me to do it?" While not much of a romantic, even Bryce had standards.

"You idiot. Don't you see? I thought I waited this long because I was afraid. That's only partly true. Do you know the real reason I waited, Bryce?"

He shook his head, unable to speak. Surely he wasn't afraid to hope?

"I was waiting for the right man." In case he retained any doubts, she made it clear. "I was waiting for you." The statement hit him a second before her shirt did. The fabric, still warm from her skin, slid down and revealed her standing tall and proud, bra cupping her breasts, skirt hanging off her hips. Moist lips beckoned, and she looked wanton with her hair tumbling over her bare shoulders, the silky strands tickling her breasts.

The glass of whiskey hit the desk. He stood and wasn't even aware of moving until he'd swept her into his arms.

Still, he hesitated. "Are you sure? I might be a pauper by tomorrow, with nothing to give."

"Don't you get it yet? I don't care about the money. I just want you. Don't you want me?" The fear he would reject her again quavered in the words.

Like fuck. He might not have an inheritance, but he couldn't turn her away. He was too selfish for that. Bryce wanted Melanie. They'd make it work.

He swept her into his arms, dipping his head until he could slant his mouth across hers. Her breath caught, and he inhaled the small sound as he kept kissing, plastering her body against his, lifting her off the floor to bring her closer. With a sound of pleasure, her lips parted, allowing him to fully taste her. Their tongues twined, and her hands crept to grip his shoulders.

He moved until her ass hit the edge of his desk. Papers and pens went crashing to the floor as he swept it clear. He parked her on it and pushed his body between her legs, never letting his lips lose contact with hers.

With her perched, he could now easily stroke her body, his calloused hands skimming her soft skin, drawing murmurs of excitement and shivers.

His fingers threaded her hair and tugged her head back, exposing her throat. First, though, he let his lips travel to the shell of her ear where he whispered, "You're mine, kitten."

"For how long?" she replied just as softly.

"Forever," was his growl before he tugged at her lobe with his teeth.

A groan rolled out of her, and he rumbled in reply. She responded so well to his touch. Shivering and moaning with everything he did.

He bent her back and let his lips burn a path from her ear to her neck then lower still to the valley between her breasts, a gorgeous handful hidden by her bra. The clasp between them gave easily and parted, displaying her perfection.

With one hand, he cupped the soft peach. His thumb brushed over the peak, and it puckered. How tempting.

He didn't resist. He sucked her nipple and part of

her breast into his mouth, suctioning and tugging while soft mewls of pleasure panted past her lips.

There was no doubt she enjoyed it. The musky aroma of her arousal surrounded him. The heat in her body rose. And she shivered, shivered and trembled and moaned at his touch.

A nip of her nipple caused a louder moan, and the guttural sound made him fucking hard.

He just wanted to sink into her. To fuck her until she screamed his name.

But he couldn't. Not yet. This was her first time. A moment she would always remember, and he had to make it good.

He had to make it epic.

As his hands skimmed over her body, his mouth returned to capture her lips. She wasn't shy and hesitant now. She clung to him fiercely, sucking his tongue, her fingers dancing along his skin.

She'd changed from her track pants to a skirt, a loose one that rose easily up her thighs until he encountered the edge of her panties. His fingers dipped around the edge, and she froze.

He froze as well. He didn't say anything, just waited.

Waited for permission.

"Don't stop."

He almost came at her reply. Instead, though, he knelt between her legs, her position on the desk the perfect height for what he had in mind. He tugged at her panties, dragging them down until they fell to the floor.

The scent of her was like a drug, making him throb with need. Hunger for a taste. Yet despite his eagerness, he remained in control, aware this was new for her. He began by teasing her, rubbing the bristled edge of his jaw along the silken skin of her inner thigh.

She gasped.

Again he rubbed, this time on the other side.

Another noise escaped her, and a fine tremor shook her body.

He blew warmly against her sex, and she moaned. "Please."

A simple word that meant everything.

He latched onto her sex with a suddenness that made her whole body arch. "Bryce!" His name emerged from her lips, part surprise, mostly pleasure.

And then she could only moan as he licked her. Licked and lapped at her sex, spreading her silken lips to truly taste her honey.

Sweeter even than maple syrup.

After a bit of licking, he moved to her pleasure nub, gripping it with his lips, giving it a tug.

That earned him a scream, and her fingers gripped his hair painfully.

Perfectly.

She was close now. So close.

He flicked her clit with his tongue, back and forth,

lashing her with it, feeling her body tighten, coiling with pleasure.

Then, he penetrated her with a finger, two of them to the knuckle.

She was fucking tight and hot.

And pure. He noted the membrane but didn't push past it. Just let his fingers pump in and out as his tongue worked her until she came.

She came hard, her whole body frozen in a bowed arc, her mouth open wide but soundless.

A powerful climax that took a moment before it ripped a loud scream from her. The mouth of her sex spasmed around his fingers, and his cock throbbed.

How good would that feel wrapped around him?

He couldn't wait to find out, and yet as he stood, ready for the next round of seduction, he stopped.

Something's not right.

The wild side of Bryce recognized the danger before he did. Smelled the smoke. Fresh smoke, not the residual sooty traces.

Melanie, her eyes still heavy with passion, confirmed it a second later. "I think the place is on fire."

Chapter 20

Melanie almost screamed! Not true. She did scream, in pleasure, but now she wanted to do it again, this time in frustration. So close to finally losing her damnable cherry, yet once again, fate intervened.

Smoke curled under the seam of the door, and she was all too aware they were on the second floor—with only one set of stairs out of here.

She popped off the desk, her skirt falling down to cover her lower body. Her bra hung over her shoulder still. She fumbled together the clasp as Bryce dared to open the door and peek outside.

He cursed. "Fuck me. The place is on fire again."

Slam. The door shut, and he whirled to face her. "We won't be getting out that way."

The bottom of her stomach fell out. "Can we leave through the window?" It seemed large enough, but the second-story jump, a jump forty feet in the air given the factory's first level needed room, meant a far fall.

"We can, but it will hurt."

"What are we going to do?" They couldn't take long to decide. The fire would spread quickly.

For a moment, Bryce eyed the bottle of whiskey, to the point she thought she'd have to explain why fire and alcohol didn't mix.

He turned from it, and his expression brightened. "There's a bathroom up here."

"How does that help us?" She did have to pee but didn't see how that would prove useful.

"I need to borrow your shirt." Before she replied, he snared it off the floor and stripped his own off before entering the room to the side, and he emerged with both of them a moment later, sopping wet.

"Go and soak your skirt," he advised.

Rather than waste breath and time asking why, she trusted in him having a plan and did as he asked, lifting the hem and spraying herself as well as she could.

When she returned, he held out the wet shirt. "Hold this over your nose and mouth. It will filter most of the smoke. We need to move fast."

So he claimed, yet he went into the bathroom once more, and she heard banging.

Clang. Clang. Whoosh.

Water sprayed out from the doorway as he emerged, wet looking and grim. The broken pipe soon shot liquid across the floor. It didn't seem enough to help, but then again, who knew? They could use any aid at this point.

"Ready?" He laced his hand in hers before the door.

No. She nodded.

He opened it, and a wave of smoke hit her in the face. The shirt over her mouth prevented her from sucking in a lungful, but her eyes stung.

Good thing Bryce held on to her because she could see nothing in the smoky haze filling the air. He knew where to go, though, and when she stumbled on the first step, he lifted her into his arms and carried her down.

She tucked her face against him, ignoring the crackle of the fire, the sting of the smoke, the terror making her heart beat too fast.

She heard an odd sizzling sound and found it less than reassuring that the water pouring down from above was turning into steam.

Bryce kept his stride steady and only cursed once when the heat licked at them unbearably. No need for waxing. The hair on her arms and legs disintegrated.

The nightmare inferno seemed like it would last forever. The heat dried out her skin, and the wet cloth grew warm. Suddenly, fresh air hit her skin, and she opened her burning eyes to see they'd made it outside. Stars twinkled above. The smell of smoke combined with that of a nearby forest, and diesel fumes. Parking lots tended to retain a certain scent.

Opening her eyes, she saw a few tanker-type vehicles. Maple syrup by the ton. Her feet hit the ground, and yet Bryce kept his arm around her. His body tensed. He also didn't move despite the heat pouring at their backs.

"We aren't alone," he murmured.

She turned her head quickly and noted someone on the edge of the pavement. Standing by a little red sports car, a pack of wolves by his side. The same wolves as the forest, the ones who attacked her.

"Isn't that Rory?" she said.

"It is." Bryce looked peeved.

Rory took a few strides forward, thumbs tucked in the loops of his jeans. "Imagine meeting you here."

"Yeah, imagine that, especially given the factory is closed. Which means you and your buddies are trespassing."

Rory held up his hands. "Getting a little hostile there, aren't you? We were just passing through."

"The same way you were passing through the woods when your pals accosted Melanie?"

For a moment Rory looked surprised. "I don't know what you're talking about."

"Bullshit. Your thugs attacked her in the forest."

Rory turned to look at his pack and for a moment, just a moment, Melanie could have sworn he seemed angry. But it passed and he shrugged. "I'm sure they were just playing with her."

"The same way they played with matches and set the factory on fire?" Bryce jabbed a finger behind them at the burning building.

"You can't prove it."

"Actually, I'll bet the surveillance footage will."

"Doesn't matter what it shows. This is my heritage."

Bryce stiffened. "The factory isn't yours yet."

"But it will be. I am, after all, Theo's son." Spoken with a sneer.

"I don't care what the tests say. No son of Theo would kill someone in cold blood." Or burn down a maple syrup factory. The horror of it.

For a moment, Rory's face took on a troubled expression, a look quickly washed away. "The factory was supposed to be empty."

"Guess again, asshole. You almost killed us both."

"Almost. But look at you, still the luckiest bastard alive." Rory said, his disgruntlement clear.

"Why are you burning it down?" Melanie's soft question entered the tension filled air.

Rory shrugged. "Because I can."

"You're fucking insane," Bryce exclaimed.

"Not insane, angry." The voice, unexpected in this place and moment, emerged from the shadows a moment before the old man did. Bryce's grandfather, Theo, casually dressed and his expression sad spoke. "I guess your mother told you. You know the truth."

"Yeah, she spoke to me. Told me that you loved this damned factory more than her." Said belligerently.

"It was more complicated than that," Theo said. "We were both married. My daughter needed me."

"My mother needed you. Do you have any idea of how my father treated her? Ignoring her. Acting so fucking cold. And I never knew why. Never even guessed until she finally told me a few weeks ago. You seduced her and then left her. You left her pregnant with your baby to face my father."

"I never knew about the pregnancy."

Rory snorted. "As if you couldn't guess when I came along nine months later."

"I swear, I never knew, or I would have done something."

"Sure you would have." The sarcasm dripped richly from his words. "Well, guess what, daddy dear. Not all of us are pussies when it comes to acting, and some of us don't think factories are more valuable than people." Rory swept a hand at the raging inferno. "This is what I think of your legacy. Soon to be my legacy. When I take over the company, I'm going to dismantle every single one of them."

"Who says you'll take over?" Theo asked the question, and Bryce stiffened.

"It's already happening. Or hadn't you heard about the hostile takeover?"

"You don't have enough shares," Theo proclaimed.

"Not yet. But I will. As soon as you die, this will be mine."

"Not according to my will," Theo announced.

But Rory wasn't daunted. "I'll contest your will as your most direct living heir."

"Except I'm not dying." Theo stood tall.

"Are you sure of that? A man your age doesn't need much to suffer a heart attack or worse." Rory didn't say a word, and yet the wolves at his side leapt forward. If they thought they would have an easy task of taking down an old man, they were mistaken.

Melanie could only watch as Theo turned into a grayer version of Bryce. His rack extended magnificently, the body showing signs of age, but still lean and strong. Theo, the moose, bent his mighty rack and tossed the wolves. However, there were three, all trying to converge in different directions.

A wild bellow from behind. and a second later another moose galloped past, joining the battle, the pair of them making short work of the snarling canines, sending them howling into the woods.

Rory, his face full of rage—and hurt—shook his fist at them. "This isn't over." He jumped into his car and took off in a squeal of tires.

As his taillights winked out of sight, the sound of sirens filled the air with a mighty wail. She waved her hands at the moose. They'd never have time to change and find clothes.

"Go. Shoo. I got this."

The sirens grew louder, and Bryce trotted close. He knelt down, offering her his back.

She could only hope a video of her riding Bryce wouldn't surface on the internet. While not a knight on a white stallion galloping away, he had rescued her while the factory burned bright behind them.

Chapter 21

Bryce made it back to the mansion, and they were all clean and Theo was in bed and looking pale when the cops arrived.

Pretending ignorance, his grandfather answered the questions. Mainly, did Theo know where Rory had gone?

Apparently, there was security footage of him breaking into the factory before the fire started and disrupted the feed. In spite of the evidence, Grandfather refused to see him charged with arson.

"The boy deserves his anger," Theo explained once the officers left.

Bryce couldn't help a curl of his lip. "Because he's your son."

"He is, and at the same time, he isn't." Theo sighed. "He might carry some of my genes, but we never had that chance to bond. He calls another father. Which is why you'll still be my main heir."

"What?" Bryce thought he'd misunderstood. Could soot make a man deaf?

"I'm not stupid. I know all the hard work you've put into this place. All the sweat. It wouldn't be right to leave it to a stranger, even if he is my blood. That doesn't mean I'll leave Rory in the cold, but the company is yours, if you still want it."

A man who'd gone to the best schools, Bryce managed an eloquent, "Duh."

"Then I guess that's settled. Which means you don't have to keep pretending with the girl. I know your relationship is a sham."

Bryce narrowed his gaze. "What happened to 'I'm dying, you need to produce an heir?'"

A shrug rolled the old man's shoulders. "I might have exaggerated a little. Which means you can call it off. I won't force you."

Bryce felt more than saw Melanie stiffen. After all they'd been through, she needed to understand something. "What if I want to stay with her?" She gasped. He turned to face her fully. "Our relationship might have started out under false pretenses, but I love you, kitten. I want to be with you."

"Really?" she exclaimed softly.

"Yes, really. You're the one for me, kitten." Not exactly how he'd imagined announcing it, with his grandfather looking on, and his bed on the other side of the house.

Clap. "This is excellent news," his grandfather declared. "When's the wedding?"

"Right now, unless he'd rather die for defiling my daughter." A certain grizzled lynx stalked into the room ahead of the disheveled butler.

"Daddy? What are you doing here?"

"I couldn't find you so I went looking. Heard there was trouble at the factory so checked there first. When I caught your scent but didn't see you, I figured you'd be here with *him*." Said with a curled lip. "Care to explain what happened to your clothes?" The pointed glare at her oversized shirt—not her own—had her blushing.

Bryce stepped in front of her. "My intentions toward her are honest."

"Good. That means you won't mind making it legal, too. Have I mentioned that I'm certified by the good ol' Internet to perform marriages? So where do you want to get this done?" Kieran pinned him with a golden gaze.

"Now?" The squeak must be a relic from some ancient rodent ancestor because a moose certainly wouldn't make that sound.

A moose also should stand by his intentions and, despite the settings and the lack of finery, do the right thing.

Why am I freaking? This is what I want.

He dropped to a knee in front of Melanie. "Kitten, I know we've not known each other long, but I need you in my life and by my side. Will you do me the honor of being my wife?"

"Yes!" Which was how they were married that same night—with Grandfather and Kendrick as witnesses—dressed in borrowed finery, Bryce in a tux his granddad loaned him and Melanie in the dress Bryce's own mother wore for her wedding dug out of the attic.

It was perfect and beautiful. Kendrick even shed a stoic tear. The ring was the family one, passed down among the generations, and it fit her finger perfectly.

When the ceremony was over and the food brought out, they didn't stay long to celebrate, especially once Kieran and Theo opened up an old bottle of scotch and began to trade barbs.

Sweeping Melanie into his arms, Bryce practically flew up the stairs to his room and had only just slammed the door shut when his lips claimed hers in a scorching kiss.

Frantic with need, hers as great as his, their hands tore at clothing, frenzied and clumsy. Her mouth clung hotly to his while moans and erratic caresses fired his blood. His cock swelled hard enough to burst.

Once they'd managed to shed their clothes, he toppled them onto the bed, skin to skin, the touch of it electrifying. Despite knowing she was new at this, he couldn't seem to slow down, not when she kissed him so passionately and groped him so thoroughly.

He lay top her, her legs parted, allowing him to settle between. Her fingers dug into his shoulders as she pressed her lips hard against his. Their open mouths meant their tongues could slide against each other.

He could have kissed her forever, but her hips wiggled under him, impatient with desire.

Tearing his mouth from hers, he caressed his way down to a tempting puckered nipple. He latched on, and his cock jerked when she cried out.

He sucked at a taut peak, drawing it into his mouth, worrying it with his teeth. While he played with her succulent breasts, he let his hand travel, looking for her moist core.

Heated honey met his fingertips, and it was his turn to moan against her flesh as he rubbed her slick cunt.

Lick it. Taste it. He could not resist the allure of her nectar. He held her down as she bucked and thrashed, his tongue torturing her tender flesh until he drew that first orgasm from her.

Before it subsided he was stretching her, sliding the tip of a finger into her tight sex, as his tongue kept lapping, bringing her back to the edge, getting her ready for what would come next.

When her moans turned into breathless gasps, he

slid up her body and let the thick head of his cock nudge her moist entrance.

She chose that moment to open her eyes and stare at him. Connecting them on a deeper level than he'd imagined possible.

"Love me," she whispered.

"Always and forever." He thrust into her, knowing this part couldn't be slow.

Her body arched, not far since he had her pinned to the bed. He held his sheathed position for a moment, letting her adjust.

When she relaxed, he caught her mouth and kissed her. Kissed her softly, still not moving. He didn't move at all until she kissed him back.

Pure torture, especially considering how tight her throbbing flesh was around him.

Slowly, he stroked her, in and out, stretching her, building her pleasure, waiting for her to respond before quickening his pace. When her hips rolled in rhythm with his strokes, he thrust even faster, her whimpering cries building in intensity.

Her body tightening as she got closer.

And closer.

"Yes!"

He didn't need her scream to feel her orgasm rippling around his cock, drawing forth his climax as she fisted him and milked him until he collapsed atop her.

And then they heard it.

Singing.

Drunken singing.

As if that stopped him from making love to his wife again.

He also later posted an update on his social media: #gotmarried.

Ping.

Melanie tagged his post: #thisrackismine.

Epilogue

A FEW DAYS LATER, IN THE MIDST OF PACKING TO visit her father's home...

Melanie paused and turned to peek at Bryce over her shoulder. He lounged on the bed, hands laced behind his head, wearing only pants and a grin.

"Excuse me, did I just hear you say you put your grandfather in a nursing home?" She blinked at him. "He's not dying. Heck, he's not even senile."

"Yeah, but the nurses and doctors don't know that. I might have given them a file saying he suffered from dementia and delusions he was a moose. Ridiculous of course."

"You put him in a human nursing home?" she squeaked.

"One for the mentally challenged with high fences and locked facilities, for their safety of course."

"Of course," she snickered. "You do know that won't hold him for long."

"I do, but after the stunt he pulled faking his illness to blackmail me into settling down, there had to be consequences. And during the time he's gone, I'm completely in charge."

"I know that glint. You're planning something devious."

"I prefer the term stunningly clever."

"And it has to be done now, before he hands over the reins?" she asked, brow arched.

"The sooner, the better, and what better time than now when we need to rebuild? The company is expanding into bacon."

"You've been dipping yours in syrup again, haven't you?"

"Don't judge me."

But she did. She judged her billionaire to be the most awesome man she'd ever met. The moose she loved. The man who would be a father to the child in her belly.

And it might be petty, but she knew he'd appreciate it. She whispered later that night, as she placed her hand on her flesh, over their babe, "We won."

SO FUCKING GLAD I DIDN'T WIN.

Rory wasn't the type to ever want to settle down. The charade had gone on for ridiculously long. Longer than he liked. It had created a clingy situation with Chanice.

He hated clingy.

He also hated the fact that he now had two fathers. Both real in different senses. Both of them pissing him off with their demands.

Screw them both. He went to Vegas to cleanse his mind before heading home to his beach house on the coast.

Played roulette and won tons of money he didn't need. Drank his face off too.

At one point, Rory woke up in the honeymoon suite, alone but for a rumpled bed and a torn pair of panties.

A few weeks later, he received an invoice for a quickie marriage done at the Chapel of Latter Day Aliens.

Blink.

He might not remember much from that night but did vaguely recall yelling, "I fucking do."

Oh shit, what did I do?

Stay tuned for the next exciting story by Eve Langlais coming in 2018: The Wolf's Secret Vegas Bride

Or check out more Eve books at EveLanglais.com